The Grinch That Stole My Heart

TN Jones

This book is a work of fiction. Names, characters, places, and incidents either are products of the author's imagination or are used fictitiously. Any resemblance to actual persons, living or dead, events, or locales is entirely coincidental.

Acknowledgment

First, thanks must go out to the Higher Being for providing me with a sound body and mind in addition to having the natural talent of writing and blessing me with the ability to tap into such an amazing part of life. Second, thanks most definitely go out to my Princess. Third, Tyanna Coston, Tyanna Presents, and Shanice B. Fourth, to my supporters who have been rocking with me from day one and to new readers for giving me a chance.

Truth be told, I wouldn't have made it this far without anyone. I truly thank everyone for rocking with me. Muah! Y'all make this writing journey enjoyable. I would like to thank everyone from the bottom of my heart for always rocking with the novelist kid from Alabama no matter what I drop. Y'all have once again trusted me to provide y'all with quality entertainment. I hope y'all enjoy, my loves!

Chapter One

Fernando "Grinch" Rogers

Thursday, November 29ᵗʰ, 2018

"Shid, Cuz, turn that shit up," Colby stated as he bobbed his head along to Eightball & MJG featuring Tela's "Sho' Nuff".

As I placed the radio's remote control in my hand and tugged on the blunt, my cell phone vibrated in my lap. Taking a quick glance at my screen, I saw my woman's name displaying across the screen. At the sight of her name, my dick was on brick mode. As I answered the phone, a wicked grin was plastered on my light-skin face.

"What yo' sexy ass want, guh?" I asked Zariah while passing the blunt to Colby.

"I wanted to know whether you're coming over for dinner?"

"Shid, what you cookin'?"

"Whatever you want to eat."

"See, that shit right there is the reason why a nigga ain't did you dirty," I replied seriously, even though I had a smile on my face.

Colby burst out laughing followed by saying that I was a fool.

"Fernando Rogers, don't play with me. I will fuck your ass up," she quickly spoke in a matter-of-fact tone before saying, "Any-damn-ways, what yo' mean ass want to eat tonight?"

"Outside of you?" I asked naughtily.

The line went silent, causing me to laugh and call her name.

"Huh?" she sexily replied.

"If you can huh you can hear, guh."

"Um, yeah, nigga, I heard you. You just caught me off guard with your comment."

"So, answer my question."

"You know damn well you don't eat no pussy, so go on 'head with that shit. I don't have time to be all psyched about you putting those juicy, light-brown lips on my hairless pussy. Now, back to dinner ... what do you want?"

"Surprise me."

"I'll do that. As usual, dinner starts at seven. You are responsible for dessert."

"Shid, this dick gon' be dessert." I blurted out, causing her and Colby to laugh.

"See, let me go because you on some more bullshit right now." She giggled.

"I'mma pick Jeremy up from daycare. So, you can rest up. Issa long ass night wit' me."

"Okay. Make sure he's wrapped up good. It's wet and cold out there. And as far as us having a long night, that's a no-no. You know I have to work tomorrow."

Making a smacking noise with my lips, I roughly said, "Mane, you ain't got no sick days you can use? I ain't trying to go to sleep until eight tomorrow moanin'."

"I'm not about to be running from you until eight in the morning. I'm only going to be running from that dick until midnight, and then I'm going to sleep."

"I guess I can take your offer."

"You don't have a choice," she quickly replied before saying, "I just called to see what you wanted to eat for dinner. I'll see you when you come over."

"A'ight."

"Bye."

That damn woman knew I hated when she tried to end our conversation with a bye; I felt as if she did that shit to get a reaction out of me.

"Mane, don't fuckin' play wit' me, guh. You know I hate when you say that word. Now, end the call properly, MaZariah Chloe Nash," I snarled as Colby handed me the blunt.

Laughing, she said, "I had to pull the Grinch out for a minute."

"Shid, you better leave that side of me alone."

"Yes, sir, Zaddy. I'll see you later."

"Now, that's more like it," I told her before saying, "A nigga got love fo' you, woman."

"And a woman got love for you, nigga," she cooed, causing a huge grin to be on my face.

As soon as I placed my phone in my lap, Colby started talking that nonsense about jumping in a more serious relationship with Zariah.

"I told you, nigga, I ain't ready fo' all that. Zariah an' I are fine just the way that we are. She ain't goin' nowhere, an' I ain't either. She knows I ain't ready fo' marriage, an' she cool wit' that."

"Mane, you sound dumb as hell. Y'all be doing relationship shit wit' a whole son out here in these streets. You stupid as fuck if you think Zariah don't want to have yo' last name. Y'all been off an' on since junior high school. Been in each other's faces since the first grade or som' shit like that. You think she stickin' 'round because of the sex? If you do, then you are one crazy ass nigga, fo' real."

Sighing heavily, I knew that Zariah wasn't sticking around for our son and our bomb ass sex life. I knew she wanted more from me, but I wasn't ready. Even though I had mad feelings for the nutmeg brown, short, sexy broad ever since we were in grammar school, that didn't move me to bend on one knee and ask shawty to marry me. I had a lot of forgiving and learning to do before I made a big step like that.

"Aye, mane, I'm finna get up outta here. Tomorrow, we'll smoke my crib out," Colby stated as his phone rang.

"Shid, I ain't gonna be able to make it. Let's make it fo' Wednesday or som' shit like that," I told him as he answered his phone, nodding his head and standing.

"What you talkin' 'bout now, Nene?" he questioned, laughing.

By the way he laughed, I knew that my cousin's baby momma was grilling his ass out for something. My nosy ass didn't want him to leave because I had to know what that fool had done now.

Angrily, he said, "Mane, Nene don't motherfuckin' play wit' me 'bout no shit like that. I swear you be ready fo' a nigga to hem yo' ass up. I don't give a fuck what you talkin' 'bout, guh. You pregnant ... again, so fuckin' get over it. I ain't goin' no-motherfuckin'-where, an' you already know this. What you carryin' on like this fo'? You actin' like a nigga a deadbeat dad or som' shit! Speak that abortion shit one mo' time an' I swear I'mma go off the deep end."

"Got damn, Nene, you let that nigga get yo' ass again?" I questioned loudly, surely to piss her off more.

Giving me the evil eye, my cousin flipped the bird my way before waltzing towards the door. Placing the phone on mute, that foolish dude told me, "Cuz, on life, if I don't call you 'round nine o'clock tonight, please come over to this guh crib. She righteously finna fuck me up."

"A'ight." I snickered before he walked out of the door.

That nigga didn't make it off my porch good enough before he started arguing with Nene. If I didn't know anybody else, I knew Nene, and she was giving that nigga a run for his money. She was cursing him out something awful to the point that he would be running back into my crib before going over to her house.

Counting down from twenty, I didn't make it to sixteen before my front door swung open and Colby nastily stated, "Mane, I don't know why in the fuck my stupid ass skeeted off in that damn guh. She gon' make me put my foot in her pregnant, ignant ass."

I couldn't do anything but laugh. I knew my cousin very well. As he plopped his ass on my sofa, I shook my head and laughed at the goofy nigga. I left that nut sitting on the sofa mad as hell and talking shit. I didn't have time to be dealing with him and Nene. I had to get myself ready for my night with my lady and our son.

Dipping into my room, Colby yelled, "So, yo' ass ain't gon' sit an' hear me vent?"

"Fuck no. I ain't got time to hear that same speech. You might as well get ready to be in the doghouse," I told him as I snatched my favorite gun from the dresser.

Strolling back into the front room, I looked at the clock and it read three-thirty. It was time to pick my chunky, spoiled six-month-old son up from daycare. Grabbing my keys off the counter table, I moved towards the stove and flipped on the light. I was sure that Colby wasn't staying at my crib since he knew I wasn't liable to come back.

Ring. Ring. Ring.

Pulling my phone off the holster, a name displayed on my phone's screen—from a worrisome broad. Sighing heavily while shaking my head, I answered.

"Yeah," I blankly voiced, walking towards my front door.

"What you doing, sexy?" Maleeka Harriot asked.

"What you want?"

"You," Maleeka cooed.

"Mane, you know it ain't that type of party wit' me. So, what do you really want?" I stated in an annoyed tone.

Smacking her lips together, Maleeka harshly said, "I need a gram of that gas."

"A'ight. Be on the lookout fo' Colby."

"Why you can't bring it?" she whined.

"You want the gram or not?" I asked nastily.

"Yeah. Tell Colby I'll be at my momma 'nem crib," she replied, salty at the realization I wasn't bringing it to her.

"A'ight," I voiced before ending the call.

"Let me guess, I gotta drop som' weed off to Maleeka."

Nodding my head, I said, "Yep. She said she'll be at her momma spot. The bitch might want som' pills, too. You can take my stash an' keep the money."

With a raised eyebrow, Colby didn't say a word as he glared into my face. When he didn't say anything, I took it upon myself to tell him that I was done dealing with the streets on that level.

"You really going to leave this easy money behind fo' a nine to five?"

"Yeah, I am. Mane, I got a son an' I don't want him growin' up seein' me in the streets or worse... dead because I don' caught a bullet that wasn't meant fo' me. You know anythin' liable to happen. It ain't just me an' Zariah no mo', woe. We got a whole lil' one dependin' on us to do right. So, I'mma leave this shit behind. You should be doing the same thing. You finna have two kids dependin' on you an' Nene. Why do you think she just blew on yo' ass 'bout being pregnant again? It surely ain't because Colbon is three. It's because you are in these streets heavy. She's scared to parent two kids by herself. Do you blame her fo' being angry wit' you?"

Dropping his head low and sighing, he replied, "Nawl, I don't blame her."

"Do you really think Auntie an' Uncle Colby wanna see us in these streets? They didn't raise us to be sellin' drugs an' shit. They raised us to be responsible niggas wit' multiple bitches if the main one didn't act right," I stated, laughing.

"Nih, nigga, you dead ass wrong fo' that shit. If Momma would've heard you say that shit, she would've popped yo' ass upside the head." He laughed, jumping to his feet.

Chuckling, I replied, "She would've knocked my head clean off my damn shoulders, fuck you mean. Anyways, you need to buckle down an' leave the illegal shit to the fools who don't give a damn 'bout shit."

"I love that fast money, though. You know this," he replied, skipping towards my room.

There was no sense in me telling my hardheaded, younger cousin shit. I had been telling him not to get heavily involved since he found out I jugged that shit back in junior high school. Colby was the type of nigga that loved having bitches in his face, even though he wasn't going to give them an ounce of his time. He liked that street credit shit; whereas, I hated it. Many people didn't know that I sold weed and pills. My clientele were mostly females and hard-working people that dealt with manufacturing companies.

"Aye, I'm finna go. Lock up," I loudly spoke before opening the door.

"A'ight. Be safe nigga."

"You too."

Stepping into the cold, wet atmosphere, I ran towards my whip. As I unlocked my doors, I hopped in the front seat and started the engine.

Zit. Zit. Zit.

Retrieving my cell phone, I saw a notification that I had received a text. Opening the text thread, I frowned as I wondered whom the number belonged to. As I read the first three words of the text message, Colby knocked on my window.

Pulling my eyes away from my phone, I rolled the window down and said, "Yeah?"

"Are you sure that you want me to get the *whole* stash an' *keep* the money?" he inquired seriously.

"Yes, I'm sure."

"Do you know how much shit you got?"

"Yep. I want you to get rid of it all, an' *don't* re-up. Get the fuck out of the streets."

"I told you—"

"Bruh, why in the fuck do you think I'm tellin' you to sell an' keep the money ... so, yo' ignant ass can leave this shit alone," I voiced in an agitated tone.

Sighing deeply, Colby ran his hands across his clean-shaven, long-shaped, light-skin face before saying, "Cuz, I got move off these streets right now."

"An' why not, Colby?"

"Because I owe them Forge boys one-hunnid an' thirty grand."

"What!" I yelled, throwing my phone on the passenger seat.

"Chill, Cuz, chill. This stash you gave me is half of what I owe them. I'm pullin' som' sideline shit just to keep my head on my shoulders."

Shaking my head, I inhaled deeply before I found the will punch him in the face followed by whooping his ass. Out of all the shit that I had told Colby not to do, he did the complete opposite.

"Don't worry 'bout nothing, Grinch. I'mma come out this shit clean. I promise you that," he said as my phone rang.

Snatching it off the seat, I didn't look at the screen because my eyes were placed on my foolish, hardheaded cousin.

"Hello," I angrily spoke into the phone.

"Don't send Colby over to my house," Maleeka stated in a low tone.

"Well, you won't get that gram you want because I ain't comin' over there."

"That's fine. I'll get it elsewhere. But um, you need to know that the Forge boys don' put a ticket over Colby's head."

"What! How much?" I inquired, angrily as I opened my car door.

"Five stacks."

"Mane, you got to be shittin' me right nih," I voiced in pure disbelief.

"No, I'm not. I gotta go. Poboy calling me."

"A'ight. Thanks fo' the heads up."

"No problem."

Maleeka was well-known in the trap world. She had a thing for dope boys, regardless of how much money they had. She knew every move they were going to make. That ghetto bitch had a great way of getting valuable information. She allowed the dope boys to stash product at her crib for a small fee.

Glaring at my dumb ass cousin, I said, "I swear if I didn't love yo' stupid ass I would put a bullet in yo' damn head. Maleeka just told me that them Forge boys don' put a five thousand dollar ticket over yo' head. Get yo' dumb ass in my whip an' go get a room in Clanton. Don't tell no-fuckin'-body where you at. Call me the second you get the room."

"Cuz, you think I'm finna run from this shit?" he laughed before continuing, "Then you really don't know me. I ain't scared of no fuckin' ticket over my head. Shid, I can give these niggas the wor—"

I shoved him against my car door and growled through clenched teeth, "At the moment, you ain't talkin' to Fernando, you are talkin' to the fuckin' Grinch! Give me yo' motherfuckin' keys, lil' nigga."

Seeing that I meant business, Colby gave me his keys and hopped in the driver's seat of my vehicle as I snatched the work from him. I didn't waste any time running back into my crib. I had to get my guns and the "for the hard times" dope that I had hidden in the second bedroom's closet. Locking and closing the door, I ran towards my cousin rose-gold, Escalade which sat on thirty-inch, gold rims.

As I took a seat in the truck and started the engine, I dialed Zariah's number. On the fifth ring, she answered.

"Aye, baby, I need you to meet me at Uncle Chun's crib."

"Why? What's goi—?"

"Zariah, I don't have time fo' the fuckin' questions an' shit. Get yo' ass to Uncle Chun's house now!"

"Okay. I'm leaving home now," she spoke in a worried tone.

"A'ight. See you soon."

"See you soon," I replied before ending the call.

"Fuck, Colby! I ain't tryin' to be in these streets like this. I got a whole fuckin' family I ain't tryin' to leave behind!" I yelled as I aggressively reversed his truck as I saw him leaving my neighborhood.

Lord, don't let these niggas shoot this fool's truck up, thinkin' it's him inside, I thought as my phone rang.

With my phone in my lap, I answered the call from Poboy.

"What up?" I spoke in a deep baritone, angry voice.

"Shit. I need to holla at you real quick like."

"Talk to me."

"Out of respect fo' you, I gotta let you know that we put a ticket over ya cousin Colby's head. We ain't wanna do it but that nigga played us out our money on one too many occasions, an' on the strength of you, we gave that nigga too many chances to make up fo' his fuck up."

"I got what he owe you."

"Um, do you know how much he owes us?"

"Yeah, a hunnid an' thirty bands."

"Hell nawl. That nigga owe us two hunnid an' thirty bands."

"What the fuck? Nigga, you gon' have to explain to me how in the fuck y'all let that nigga run up a tab like that."

"We ain't let him run up shit. Colby volunteered to do a run to Texas with two-hunnid an' thirty g's worth of product. Halfway to the drop off spot, that dumb ass nigga got pulled over by twelve an' fled."

With an angry facial expression, I growled before saying, "I ain't gon' let you knock my cousin off the map. I got som' shit that should put y'all well over the amount that he lost y'all. When an' where you wanna meet up?"

"Bingo Hall on Atlanta Highway in fifteen minutes," he stated.

"Bet," I replied before ending the call.

This shit with Poboy is not finna be a walk in the park. Stupid ass Colby don' put me back in the game knowin' damn well this shit almost cost Zariah her sanity. How in the fuck am I going to explain this shit to her without her wantin' to leave an' take our son from me? On life, I'mma make Colby suffer.

MaZariah "Zariah" Nash

"Oh my God! Fernando, stop it!" I yelled as he slammed Colby against the table inside of the hotel room.

"I told yo' ass a long time ago to leave that shit alone, Colby. Do you know what the fuck you just cost me today? My fuckin' sanity," Fernando spoke through clenched teeth as he backed away from his bloodied-face cousin.

"I told you ... I had shit under control, Grinch. I ain't tell you to step in an' handle a motherfuckin' thing! You did that shit on yo' own free will. You cost yo' own sanity, nigga!" Colby loudly voiced as he shoved Fernando into the dresser that held a flat screen Sony T.V.

For fifteen minutes, I tried my best to break up the fighting cousins. My voice was strained as I spoke loudly for them to cut the madness out. I had no idea what Colby had done, but it had to have been bad because it had been a long time since I'd seen the "Grinch" side of Fernando.

Once Fernando had Colby in a chokehold, harshly talking to him, I had to intervene before he seriously hurt him.

"That's enough, Fernando. Cut the shit out now!" I told him as I ran up to them.

"Don't fuckin' touch me, Zariah. I told you to wait in the car!" my official lover since the seventh grade growled as he placed his brown eyes on me.

"I'm not a fucking dog, Fernando! You do not talk to me like that. I said that's e-motherfuckin'-nough. He's your cousin. Whatever he's done, y'all can talk that shit out. If you don't let him go this minute, you and I will have some serious problems!" I yelled while pointing my finger in his face.

Releasing his gasping cousin out of the tight grip, Fernando glared at Colby and spat, "You know me better than any motherfucka in the streets. You know I don't play 'bout family, an' fo' a motherfucka to give me a fuckin' courtesy call 'bout placin' a ticket over yo' head put me in a position that I really didn't need to be in."

"What the fuck?" I asked, eyes wide as a sixty inch smart T.V.

"Cuz, I had shit under control. Them niggas wasn't gon—" Colby stated before Fernando jumped in his face.

"Poboy called me his motherfuckin' self an' told me that he put a ticket over yo' head, you fuckin' idiot. I been told you to leave that shit alone an' that I could get you a position at my job, mane. I ain't got time to be buryin' you. You need to wise the fuck up. I'm tired of talkin' to you, Colby. You ain't my son, an' yet I gotta keep repeatin' my-damn-self to you."

"Then, stop talkin', nigga. Apparently, I ain't listenin'." Colby shot back.

Fernando raised his fist, and I caught it. "Let's go. You can't beat him into listening to you, baby. Please let's go."

Ring. Ring. Ring.

My cell phone rang, and I ignored it. Fernando was ready to pounce on his cousin, and I wasn't going to let him beat on Colby anymore. I saw enough to know that my son's father had a death look in his eyes.

My phone stopped ringing, only to start back. I retrieved my phone and saw Nene's name on the display screen.

"Colby, Nene is calling me. If she asks if I've seen you, what do I need to tell her?"

"The fuckin' truth ... you are starin' this dummy in the face. Wit' his stupid ass," Fernando spoke as he retrieved a blunt from his pocket.

"That you haven't seen me today," Colby sighed, looking at me.

Answering the phone as normal as I could, I was shaking like a stripper. My nerves were all over the place.

"Are you with Grinch?" Nene asked worriedly.

"Yeah. What's up?" I asked with my eyes on Fernando.

"I just heard that the Forge boys just removed a ticket off Colby's head, and that Grinch agreed to work with them in exchange for Colby's life. I'm so tired of Colby trying to run the streets. I'm sick of this shit. Every other month, he into some shit."

"What!" I yelled, placing my eyes on the man that I loved with every breath in my body.

"What?" Colby and Fernando stated in unison as I backed away.

Continuing, Nene said, "Grinch came to make the full payment on behalf of Colby's stupid ass, but Poboy also wanted Grinch's expertise in the streets. That nigga wants all the power, and the only person to give him that is Grinch."

Angry as hell, I said, "Nene, I'll be at your home soon to get my son."

"Zariah, do not be ma—"

"Mad isn't the fucking word right now, Nene. I gotta go, but I'm leaving where I'm at now to come get Jeremy," I told her with my eyes locked on the man that vowed he was done with the streets.

"Okay."

Without a moment's hesitation, I quickly ended the call and cocked my head to the right. So many things were going through my head until it was unbelievable. I pondered why Fernando didn't find another way to resolve things with Nene's want-to-be notorious cousin.

As I analyzed the handsome monster in front of me, he said, "Let me guess, Nene told you 'bout the agreement between her cousin an' me?"

"What agreement?" Colby asked, looking between his cousin and me.

Ignoring Colby, I hurtfully asked, "Why did she have to tell me? That was supposed to have been your fucking job. You thought I wasn't going to find out, *Grinch*?"

"I was going to tell you, Zariah. I just had to whoop on this fool's head first. I would never hide anythin' from you. You know this," he said while firing up the blunt.

"Too bad I don't feel that way. You had plenty of chances to tell me, but you chose not to. I told you what would happen if you chose the streets over us, and I meant that," I told him, turning towards the door.

"Zariah! Don't you walk yo' ass out that fuckin' door!" Fernando yelled, not far from behind me.

"Watch me walk out this door, *baby daddy,*" I said as I slung the door open and stepped onto the wet pavement.

I didn't make it far before Fernando snatched me up and brought me back into the room. Standing against the door, he pulled me close to him. As the tears spilled down my face, I pushed him away.

"You don't push away from me, damn it."

"I do what the fuck I want to do when you think I'm something to play with!" I yelled as I slapped him across the face.

Gently grabbing my throat, he glared into my eyes and said, "Baby, I swear I didn't have a choice. When I talked to Poboy on the phone, he made it seem like he wanted the money that Colby owed. Thus, I had enough dope an' shit to cover that nigga's tab. However, when I got to the meetin' spot, that nigga changed the terms. He didn't want the money. He wanted me to join his force an' make him powerful. I have alliances that will give him exactly what he wants. Trust, I told that nigga I ain't 'bout that life anymore. That's when he threw up that he would bless me wit' a triple funeral … Colby's, Auntie's, an' Uncle Colby's."

"Oh, my God!" I exclaimed as Fernando removed his hand from around my neck.

"Aw fuck," Colby stated in a sad tone.

"Yeah, *aw fuck*. I told you that nigga would use you to get to me. I told you to leave that shit 'lone fo' this reason here, Colby. You fucked up big time, an' now I gotta clean up yo' mess. Just because you don't give a fuck 'bout yo' child wit' a new one on the way doesn't mean I don't give a fuck 'bout mine!" Fernando angrily yelled.

"I'm sorry, y'all," he voiced, apologetically.

I couldn't tell him that I forgave him or that everything would be okay. I didn't believe for a minute that things would be okay. Not my relationship with Fernando, not my sanity of having peace, and surely the situation Colby's reckless ass placed Nene in.

"Yep, that you are. One sorry motherfucka that I gotta clean up," Fernando voiced as he stood inches away from the door. "If I lose my girl an' son because of you, Colby. I will murder you my-fuckin'-self in front of Auntie an' Uncle Colby. An' that's on my fuckin' life, nigga."

***

After dinner, we showered and gave Jeremy our undivided attention. Fernando made sure to tire his chunky tail out until he could barely keep his eyes open. I loved seeing my love interacting with our son. It was the cutest, loving thing in the world. I couldn't have picked a better man to father our son. Fernando took pride in being called a dad. He went beyond caring for Jeremy. It was to the point that he barely let me do anything for our son.

When I first found out that I was pregnant, I was scared to tell Fernando. I had to critically think about the pros and cons of having him in our son's life. Even though he worked at International Papers, Fernando still sold drugs. He was a street-nigga with no manners. He talked to people—minus his loving guardians, my Nanna, Nene, Colby, and me—as if he wasn't raised to respect others. I didn't want that lifestyle or attitude around our child. I sure as hell didn't want to be a part of it.

Those were the reasons why I withheld the information of me being pregnant up until I started showing. I was trying my best to escape his love; yet, I failed miserably because I yearned to be with him. I yearned for him to leave the streets alone. It wasn't like he was hurting for money.

"What are you thinkin' 'bout?" Fernando's sexy, deep voice asked while rubbing my stomach as I lay outstretched on my dark brown, suede sofa.

"How things are going to play out for us," I replied as I looked into his eyes.

"You don't have to worry 'bout a thing. I got shit covered … trust, I do. Everyone that I love will come out unscathed. I promise you that," he voiced, slowly sliding his hand from my belly to my face.

"I don't want to be tormented every second of the day. I don't want to go through the phone calls of you being shot. I don't want to relive the past again. I can't do this, Fernando. I've been through too much with you and these streets, dating back to our ninth grade year. We are finally at peace. Hell, I'm finally at peace. No anxiety or panic attacks. Are you sure you can't find another way to satisfy what Poboy wants without being present?"

"No, I can't. This is the only way. However, I don't take kindly to threats being made to those that I love. When I say that I have a play underway, I do. It's one that will not have my family cryin'. You see, Poboy fucked up the moment he mentioned that Auntie an' Uncle Colby would die, along wit' Colby, if I didn't agree. I could've blown his brains out in the truck, but I would be sittin' in jail as we speak an' you an' Jeremy's lives would be at stake. I had to agree an' let him go, but him an' his crew won't be breathin' fo' long."

Climbing into his lap, I gazed into his eyes while rubbing his soft, wavy, jet-black beard. Words couldn't explain how much I loved the man that I lost my virginity to. There was no vocabulary word in any language that could explain how I would feel if anything happened to the man that stole my heart. He was my other half, but I knew I needed to put some space between the two of us—for the sake of our son.

"You are not takin' my son away from me, an' you sure as hell ain't leavin' me, MaZariah Chloe Nash, so you can get that thought off yo' mind, an' remove that facial expression as well." He sighed heavily, massaging my round behind.

There was no need in me debating what he said. I'd learned a long time ago not to argue with him. It wasn't going to get me anywhere.

"How long do you think it will take you to get out of this jam?"

"Three months at the most. A month in a half if things go as planned," he replied seriously, applying more pressure to my ass.

"Mm," I groaned as I dropped my forehead onto his nose.

"That feels good to that baby, don't it?" he sexily groaned before licking his juicy lips.

"Yesss," I replied as I felt the second monster waking up.

"Look at me, Zariah."

Doing as he commanded, my breathing became unsteady as I anticipated the loving from him.

"I'm *never* going to leave y'all side an' I mean that shit. Don't push me away because you know I'on like being in time out or isolation. I *need* you. I've always needed you. A nigga got mad love fo' you, an' you bet not ever forget that."

My eyes became moist as I said, "I won't."

Parting my lips with his tongue, Fernando slowly yet firmly gripped my exposed thighs. I cooed in his mouth as our tongues slow danced. Every time he kissed me, I swear I was floating on a white, puffy cloud thousands of miles away from here. I would never get used to his passionate, sloppy kisses. I would never get used to his tender touches on my body, and I sure as hell wouldn't get used to the way he dicked me down.

As we engaged in a heated kiss, Fernando placed me on my back. Opening my legs to receive him, a tingling sensation ran quickly from my head to my toes. It seemed as if I was being tased; I loved that powerful, amazing feeling.

Raining kisses on my lips while caressing my sides and thighs, I cooed, "A woman got mad love for a nigga."

Removing his lips from mine, Fernando took his time removing my panties while saying, "A nigga got stupid mad love fo' you, Zariah."

His mouth blessed my neck, the center of my slightly filled acne chest, and my size D breasts. He took his time catering to my upper torso as two of his fingers slipped into my kitty.

"Ah," I softly moaned as I began thrusting my pussy on his masterful fingers.

Placing my hands on his head, I gently massaged his large-sized dome—eager to alleviate his stress and worries from today. Fernando loved massages while we made love, and I made sure to do it every time he was inside of me.

"I need you, MaZariah Chloe Nash," he groaned, sliding his tongue into my belly button while applying pressure inside of my core.

"I need you too, Fernando Gerald Rogers," I moaned, back arching and legs trembling.

The sensation I was feeling from him was phenomenal to the point that tears streamed down my face—like always.

"I motherfuckin' need you, MaZariah Chloe Nash," he angrily growled as he removed his fingers from my kitty and replaced it with his mouth, something he'd *never* done.

"Ahhhh!" I screamed before placing my hand over my mouth.

My body shook violently as Fernando lovingly and sweetly attacked my hungry pussy. I couldn't stop my eyes from rolling in the back of my head if I wanted to. I couldn't control the muffled noises that sounded off in the palm of my hand. I wouldn't dare stop him from slurping and sucking my sweet liquids from my tunnel of love.

"Look at me!" he spat.

I poorly did what he asked of me; thus, I received a pop to my thigh as he sucked on my clit.

"I said fuckin' look at me, an' don't take yo' eyes off me." He demanded sexily with his mouth covering my girl.

"O … O … Oouuuu," I cried out as I placed my eyes on him.

For God knows how long, I watched that damn man work his fingers and mouth on me. I didn't know how many times I cried out his name or stated that I was cumming. All I knew was that Fernando Rogers had me fucking gone, and I knew that I wasn't going to be able to recover—ever!

"I'm full nih," he stated with an evil smile on his face.

I was so pleased and exhausted that I could go to sleep, but I needed the main course—that dope dick!

"May I feel you?" he whispered in my ear as he pulled down his gym shorts and boxers.

I nodded my head.

"I know that I can, but I'm askin' can I feel, feel you."

"Yess," I replied as I helped him remove his shirt.

"You do know there's a high possibility that I ain't gon' pull out, right?"

"Yes."

"An' you okay wit' that?"

"Yes an' no."

"Then, I can't feel, feel you."

"If it comes to that ... like Colby told Nene ... I will have to accept it and move the fuck on," I whimpered as I felt his fat, long tool near my tunnel of love.

Without further ado, we rocked the shit out of my sofa, the kitchen table and chairs, and finally my bed. Round after round, Fernando tore off in my ass and I loved every single moment. Each time when he was close to climaxing, he would ask me could he leave him in, and every fucking time my crazy ass told him that he could. That dick was too damn good not to be in me as his boys slipped from his balls.

With my legs on his shoulders, Fernando sweetly pounded me as he pulled my head towards his head and lovingly said, "I motherfuckin' love you, guh. I need you, an' only you. On life, I love you an' only you. Please don't leave me."

I became so emotional that I cried as he fucked me. I didn't have enough strength to reciprocate the intimacy back. For me to hear him say the word that I had been dying to hear from him, took me to a place that I always dreamt of being—overjoyed. Yeah, I knew that he loved me. Yeah, he had always said that he had mad love for me, but he'd never said I love you.

"MaZariah Chloe Nash, I love you," he cried as he began making love to me, looking into my eyes.

Crying with a face filled with happy tears, I cooed, "I love you, Fernando Gerald Rogers."

Chapter Three

Grinch

Saturday, December 1ˢᵗ

It was the time of year where family was supposed to come together in a loving environment and be merry. Shit, I was far from merry as I thought of my parents and how much they used to enjoy this time of the year. I missed them like crazy, and I wished I could see their smiling faces. I was five years old and the only child when I lost my parents to an airplane crash. They were leaving The Bahamas from celebrating their fifteenth-year anniversary.

The day Auntie Maryann and Uncle Colby Senior told me that my parents were no longer on this earth tore my little world up. I was a lost child in a battle of family members that wanted me. I came with two, large life insurance policies and a college fund that my parents had started saving for me. For a five-year-old to witness adults going at it about a child that they barely had contact with was heartbreaking—especially to Auntie Maryann and Uncle Colby. The court system got involved. I really didn't think I had any say so in the matter of whom I wanted to be with, but my small, angry voice spoke loud and clear to the family court advocate.

Without a doubt, she knew how I felt about my aunt, uncle, and three-year-old cousin, Colby.

Two months after my parents' death, my auntie and uncle became my guardians. Even though my parents lived in the same city as my aunt and uncle, I had to change schools because of where they lived. The school I had transferred to was nothing like the school I had been going to since pre-kindergarten. The all-Black school was different from the mostly White school I had become accustomed to. Instantly, I was angry and badly wanted my parents.

Every day, I acted out. I was mean, nasty, and rude just because I didn't like the way my life had turned out for me. Parent visitation days and luncheons caused me to cry myself to sleep at night. Auntie Maryann, Uncle Colby, and Colby would be by my side as I let my tears slide down my face. I angrily vented, and they comforted me. Being at school wasn't a walk in the park for me. I completed my schoolwork and anything else the teacher asked of me, but I refused to make friends or talk to anyone. I became isolated. Truth be told, I hated the kids in my classroom for bragging about what they were going to do with their parents during the weekends.

Halfway into the second semester of school, all of that changed the moment I placed my eyes on a bucktooth, nappy headed, big-eyed, pretty girl named MaZariah Nash. She was a new student from a different school out of state. When she took a seat next to me, I noticed that she was sad. I whispered to her that she would be okay, and that I would be her friend.

I was a five-year-old kid telling an unknown, sad-faced girl that I would be her friend. Who knew that that girl would remain my friend and become the mother to my son? Who would have known that the day she strolled into my kindergarten class she would change how I saw life without my parents? Not only did she change my view about them, she made me appreciate my auntie and uncle for taking me into their home and treating me with the same love that my parents bestowed upon me. Zariah was smart for her age; another reason I took to her so well.

To this day, I highly believe I fell in love with Zariah the second week of her being in my class. Whenever someone spoke about me not having parents, Zariah would get in trouble for punching them in the face or cursing them out. From then, we were thick as thieves. Whenever people saw her, they saw me and vice versa.

From the first day to the last day of middle school, I had asked her several times to be my girlfriend, and she would always smile and shake her head. She would tell me that she'd prefer that we waited before getting dating. One would feel like a fool for chasing behind their friend, but I didn't. I knew one day that she would give into me. When that day finally came, we were in the seventh grade, and she saw a big-booty, light-skinned, pretty girl with hazel-green eyes talking to me at my locker.

Zariah strolled her ass over to my locker, hooked her arm in mine, kissed me on my cheek, grabbed my dick, and told Maleeka, "Mine. All mine. Don't make me get put in in-school suspension about this one."

That was the day Maleeka was constantly at Zariah's throat about me.

Later that night, Zariah called and told me to sneak in her window around nine-thirty. I did that with a smile on my face. That lovely, wet night, we lost our virginity, and vowed that we would never sleep with anybody else.

"Fernando!" Auntie Maryann screamed over Christmas music.

"Ma'am!" I voiced loudly as I closed the refrigerator door.

When the music stopped playing, she spoke, "I know damn well you ain't in my fridge drinking out the damn juice carton!"

Laughing, I replied, "Guilty."

"I'mma beat yo' ass. I told you about that. How many times do I have to tell you about drinking out of the juice carton like that boy?"

Chuckling, Uncle Colby said, "Now, you know good and well you gonna fuss at him until he's old and gray about that. He ain't gonna stop. That's why I take pride in getting the first two cups before his suck mouth ass get over here."

"Why I gotta be a 'suck mouth ass'?" I laughed, strolling into the living room.

"Because yo' ass is," they replied, laughing.

"Boy, if you don't stop runnin' in an' out this door, yo' grandma gonna get you!" Colby yelled at Colbon.

"You better stop hollerin' at him, Colby. I would hate to box you upside yo' head," Auntie Maryann stated loudly, causing me to laugh.

"Box him out, Auntie. Box that nigga out." I laughed as Colby and Colbon walked into the living room.

"See, you always wanna see a nigga get a whoopin'. You ain't right," he spoke in a casual tone, not looking at me.

I didn't respond because if I did, Auntie Maryann and Uncle Colby would know there was strife between us. Whenever we had a fight or argument, we tried our best to keep it between the two of us. If we didn't, then they would intervene, asking questions and shit. We never told on each other; thus, it would equal ass whoopings for us.

"Are we gonna put up these decorations or not, folks? I gotta get Fat Daddy from Nanna's house, grocery shop, an' have dinner ready by the time Zariah get off work," I told them as I stood, looking at the mountain of Christmas shit we had to put up.

"Oh Lord, she trusting yo' ass to cook dinner." Auntie Maryann laughed before continuing, "Shit, the fire department will have their hands tied this evening."

"Woman, that only happened one time." I chuckled as I separated the pile of colored lights.

"Boy, them folks got called to that house seven damn times. You better off just ordering some food. Ain't nobody got time to be coming home to a smoky house," Uncle Colby stated, laughing.

"I have gotten better. Ask Colby. He don' taught me a thing or two 'bout cookin'."

"More like ten things 'bout cooking," my hardheaded cousin replied as he bent to retrieve the bottom portion of the white Christmas tree.

Thirty minutes later, we were halfway done with decorating the inside of the single-family home. The elders assigned Colby and me to start putting up decorations outside. I knew exactly what they were trying to do. You see, Colby and I weren't joking or goofing around like we normally did during holidays. We only spoke to each other when need be—just to keep them from asking questions.

"Aye, I know you got a plan fo' them niggas. What is it? I know I can help since I'm the one that put you into th—" Colby lowly voiced as he placed the air machine nozzle inside of a medium-sized snowman.

"Don't worry 'bout that. Yo' life is safe as long as you stay the fuck out of these streets. I'm not going to save you again, an' I mean that shit. The biggest favor you can do for me is ... get a damn job an' do something wit' yo' life. Don't you got another baby on the way? Ain't Nene don' left you?" I questioned nastily as I looked at him in the same manner that I had spoken.

Doing what I expected him to do—shut the fuck up—Colby continued doing his job of placing Christmas ornaments around the manicured front lawn.

As we were close to finishing our task, Auntie Maryann stood on the porch and called our names.

"Ma'am?" we replied in unison as we looked at her.

"Come here."

When we approached her, she said, "Spill the beans. Something happened between the y'all. I want details now."

"Ain't nothin' happened between us," we said, giving her our full attention.

"Y'all do know that I raised y'all little pissy asses, right?"

Laughing while nodding our heads, we responded, "Yes, ma'am."

"Then spill it."

"We ain't got nothin' to spill, Momma. Seriously," Colby spoke as I nodded my head.

"If I find out y'all lying ... I don't give a damn if y'all don't live in my house and y'all are grown ... I'm coming to whoop some ass. Understood?"

"Understood." We sounded off while saluting her, which caused her to laugh before entering the house.

Ring. Ring. Ring.

Clearing my throat as I retrieved my cell phone, I quickly glanced at the screen. Seeing one of my partners' names displaying, I told my folks that I was leaving and that I loved them. Like usual, they lovingly sent me on my way.

Excitedly growling and smiling, I answered the phone with a 'yo'.

"Aye, let's meet up at American Deli on Ann Street," Gun'em said before deeply inhaling.

"A'ight. What time?"

"Shid, nih fo' real."

"A'ight. I'm leavin' Auntie 'nem crib nih."

"Bet. Tell them I said hello."

"I will have to do that another time. I'm headed to my whip," I spoke as I walked passed Colby while he glared at me.

Chuckling, Gun'em said, "A'ight."

"I'll be there in a minute," I stated, unlocking the doors of vehicle.

"Bet," he replied, signaling that the call was at a closure.

As I climbed into the front seat, I placed my phone in the holster. Starting the engine on my vehicle, I saw Colby trying to flag me down. I acted as if I didn't see him and reversed out of my folks' yard. Before I could put the gearshift in drive, he called my phone. Ignoring the call, I shook my head at the nigga that I grew up with but whose presence I hated now. I didn't have any time to waste talking to Colby. Everything that was going on was his fault. If his hardheaded ass would've listened to me none of this shit would be popping off.

Zipping out of the residential street, I couldn't wait to sit down with Cornelius 'Gun'em' Parks and discuss how we were going to take the Forge boys out. There was no doubt in my mind that things would go exactly as we wanted them to. One thing about Gun'em, when he had his mind set on something, it would be executed just the way he had planned. If it didn't happen, he would wait until the right time presented itself.

Within six minutes, I pulled beside Gun'em's black-on-black Ford F-250. As he stepped out of his truck, a mountain of thick smoke escaped with him. That character smoked morning, noon, and night; there wasn't a day that went by that he didn't have a blunt to his lips.

"Mane, what I told you 'bout ridin' an' smokin'?" I laughed him as we walked towards the back of our vehicles.

"Shid, woe, after today's event at the doctor's office, I had no choice but to fire up one," he stated with a slight chuckle.

"What don' popped off wit' you, nigga?"

"I don' fucked 'round an' got my lil' cut-buddy knocked up. Nih she mad talkin' big shit 'bout a nigga on punishment an' all types of shit."

"The college chick, right?"

"Hell yeah."

"I'm surprised she ain't down to have yo' seed, woe," I voiced as he opened the door to the chicken joint.

"Same thing I said, but she ain't hearin' nothin' 'bout no kids at twenty. So, I gotta do somethin' to get her mind right an' on board. Dude, this will be our first kid an' I'm really diggin' her lil' nerdy, thick ass. She thinkin' that she won't be able to lock me down 'cus I'm a street nigga. I be tryin' to tell her I'm a different breed," he confessed before sighing heavily.

I knew off the top that Gun'em was taking it hard that his little shawty wasn't on board with having his baby. Most females that sincerely care about a street nigga didn't want to deal with them on that level. In the ninth grade, Zariah broke up with me when she learned where my extra money was coming from.

"You an' Colby ain't playin' 'round this holiday season, huh?" I joked as we moved closer towards the counter.

"Hell nawl. You should be up next, eh?" he asked while looking at me, showcasing a mouth filled with gold teeth.

"I'm hopin' so ... once shit die down."

"You crazy as fuck if you think Zariah going to have another baby an' Jeremy only six months old."

Lowly, I happily said, "She let a nigga in last night … raw."

"Null nih. So, she don' let y'all come off condom probation," he voiced happily while dapping me up.

Chuckling, I replied, "I hope so, but it might've been what I did to keep her from tryin' to leave me."

"You told her 'bout the situation, didn't you?" he asked while shaking his head.

"Actually, Nene spilled the beans. I wasn't going to tell her. You already know how hard it was fo' a nigga to get back into her good graces."

Nodding his head, Gun'em replied, "Oh, trust I know. You had me an' Colby beggin' her like we were Keith Sweat, woe."

Continue, he said, "Please tell me that you whooped yo' cousin somethin' good behind his stunt."

"An' you know I motherfuckin' did."

While we briefly waited to have our order taken, Gun'em asked me how he was going to get back into good graces with his little buddy. From there, we talked about our relationships and how we wanted to perfect them. Gun'em and I had a friendship like none other, dating back to our days in the fifth grade. He was the first person besides my auntie and uncle to tell me about sex. Unlike Auntie and Uncle, Gun'em went into full detail.

42

By the sixth grade, Gun'em had lost his virginity and classified himself as a sex expert. Any and everything the fellas in our circle wanted to know about sex, Gun'em was the person we would talk to. He told us which websites were the best to visit and the do's and don'ts of having sex. To this day, that educated, hood nigga was our go-to person when it came to bedroom action—especially if we wanted to spice things up on another level.

"Now, we have ate an' received knowledge on how to better our relationship ... it's time to get down to business," Gun'em lowly voiced as he wiped his mouth with a clean napkin.

For twenty minutes, we discussed the plans for the Forge boys. When our conversation ended, I didn't know who was the happiest. Strolling out the restaurant's door, we zipped towards Foot Locker. Ten minutes in the establishment, we exited with three bags apiece. Neither of us could leave a shoe store without purchasing something. Like always, we copped something for the lady in our life; I grabbed Jeremy the same shoes that I bought Zariah and me. I loved when we dressed alike; whereas, Zariah hated.

"Be easy, my nigga," Gun'em stated as he placed a cigarette to his black lips before dapping me up.

"Same to you."

Hopping into our rides, I retrieved my phone and dialed Poboy's number. On the third ring, he answered.

"I'm headed to Vaughn Park now."

"A'ight. I'm already here wit' the kids an' shit."

"A'ight. See ya' in a minute."

"Cool."

Ending the call, I started my engine with a smile on my face. Reversing away from the shopping center, I thought of the plan to knock those niggas down several notches. They wouldn't be able to recover from the hit that we were going to provide them—if any of them survived the initial massive attack.

My thoughts ceased the moment I heard Young Scooter's "Hector Story" playing. Turning the volume up to the last notch, I bobbed my head and rapped along with the song. As I cruised through the diverse community on Harrison Road, I was crunk while my speakers beat down the block. I was so amped that I did something that I rarely did, smoked and ride. I bitched my niggas out about smoking weed and riding; yet, I felt the need to face a blunt before I placed myself around a nigga that swore he was going to take over through me.

"Ayye, Ayye," I spoke as Young Jeezy's voice sounded off in "Hypnotize".

Three minutes away from the most visited park in Montgomery, I was eager to get the meeting over with. I had better shit to do than becoming halfway acquainted with a group of niggas that would never be on my level.

When I pulled into the park, I saw the Forge boys and three of the nine of Poboy's kids. Parking my whip, I hopped out and stashed my blunt inside of the ashtray. Locking the doors, I strolled towards the center of the field where they were throwing a football. Poboy nodded at me and began walking towards me.

Lexin "Poboy" Turkleson was in his late twenties. He was tall, dark-skinned, multiple tattoos on his body, and raggedy looking dreads that hung passed his shoulders. Poboy was an average Joe dressing nigga when he spent time with his kids, but once the street lights come on he was dressed in designer clothing from head to toes.

"What's up, Grinch?" they spoke as Poboy and I dapped each other up.

"Shit, coolin'," I replied as the rest of the Forge boys dapped me up.

One of the little youngin's threw me the ball, and I slung it towards him. Before we chopped it up, we played ball with the kids. Poboy excused himself from his crew and sons.

As we walked towards the track, he said, "How soon do you think your alliances would set up a meetin' wit' me?"

"If their calendar is free, soon as tomorrow."

"That's what's up. Have they told you what they would want from me?"

"I didn't ask. I was mainly interested in when they could chop it up wit' you."

"A'ight. Do you really know why I called you into this situation?"

Chuckling, I looked at the nigga as if he was retarded. "Yep because I got the alliances that will place y'all on top of the world."

Nodding his head, Poboy replied, "That an' the simple fact that you is one smart ass nigga. You know how to move shit without a motherfucka knowin'. You think we ain't heard of the stories of how you escaped gettin' yo' crib raided? You are damn near untouchable; however, I need to keep my eyes on you because I made a threat that I should've never made concernin' Maryann an' Colby Senior."

I didn't say anything as an eerie silence overcame us.

Continuing, he said, "Mane, I regret sayin' that because they looked out fo' me when my own family didn't give a fuck 'bout me. Whenever I needed a place to stay or somethin' to eat, they always welcomed me into their home. I don't want you to think fo' a second that I would harm them, an' I really don't need any bad blood between the two of us. We grew up together, got whoopin's together, an' all that shit. Grinch, I'm comin' to you as a man an' I'm askin' you somethin' that I never asked any motherfucka in my life … to forgive me fo' lettin' that horrible statement that came out of my mouth."

Stopping in my tracks, I looked into his long-oval shaped face before extending my hand and saying, "I don' told you on mo' than one occasion to never say anythin' that you would have to apologize fo' later. However, since we been down fo' a hot ass minute. This is the only time that I'm goin' to accept yo' apology."

Showcasing his gold, grilled-out mouth, we shook hands.

"You ain't got to worry 'bout me doin' no hoe shit like that again," he voiced as we continued walking.

You damn right. Yo' days are close to bein' over, fuck nigga.

We walked around the track four times, talking about what he wanted from my alliances and what he was willing to give in return. By the time we completed the fifth round on the large pavement, I looked at my phone for the time.

"I think we've had a productive talk. Do you?" I asked as I stopped in front of my truck.

"Hell yeah!" He smiled while clasping his hands together.

"I'll be in touch the moment they hit me up."

"A'ight. Be safe."

"Same to you," I replied as we dapped each other up.

Moving towards the driver's door of my vehicle, I retrieved my phone and called Nanna. On the third ring, she answered.

"I'm on the way, Nanna," I told her as I started the engine.

"Okay, baby. Will you stop by the store and get me two bags of honey roasted peanuts and a Coca-Cola?"

"Yes, ma'am."

"Thank you."

"What I told you 'bout all that thankin' me an' stuff." I joked with her.

"Boy, get yo' yella ass off my phone," she stated while laughing.

"How was Jeremy today?"

"Fernando Rogers, get yo' ass off my phone. You know I don't like doing all that talking over these phones. We'll talk when you get here."

Chuckling, I replied, "A'ight woman."

Ending the call with Zariah's grandmother, I shook my head at the woman who made it her business that we brought Jeremy to her early on Saturday mornings and picked him up around three p.m. Nanna was a laid-back, old-school woman who loved her some Zariah. She raised her as if she was her own. Thus, Nanna went above and beyond for my boy. He was her only great-grandchild and she spoiled him just as much as Zariah, Auntie Maryann, Uncle Colby, Colby, Nene, and me. If it wasn't for Nanna, Jeremy wouldn't know what it felt like to have a grandmother. Zariah's mother was a piece of shit; there was no way in hell I would allow Zariah to have our son around that woman—period.

Once I stopped by the store and picked up my son, things went in a blur. My boy babbled as we went grocery shopping. He was as handsome as I was, so we were a chick-magnet, but I shoo'ed the broads off. They weren't Zariah; thus, they got kicked to the curb real fast. Of course, they didn't like that. There had been plenty of times were bitches tried to step down on my girl, causing me to bring out a side of me that I enjoyed letting them see.

When we arrived home, it wasn't a smooth transition of getting groceries and Jeremy in the house. Zariah, Nene, and Auntie Maryann made that shit look easy as fuck. I dropped several bags, including his heavy diaper bag on the ground. Once I picked those bags up, Fat Daddy began bouncing and shit, causing more bags to fall down the four steps leading to the door.

"Come on, Jeremy. Why you always do that to me? You don't do it to yo' mother an' yo' two aunties," I stated, placing the car seat on the porch.

As I placed the keys in the doorknob, I heard a car pull into the driveway. It was Zariah. With a smile on my face, I wondered what she was doing off work.

"Look like you need some help." she laughed, stepping out of her car looking absolutely stunning as she wore her standard uniform of khaki pants and a blue Best Buy shirt.

"Yes, I do, love. What are you doin' off early?" I asked as I placed our son across the threshold of the door.

"I didn't feel like being there," she softly stated as she picked up four bags.

"Bad day being a shift supervisor?"

"Not really. A slow one. I hate slow days." She huffed, walking onto the porch.

Retrieving the bags out of her hands, I pulled her into my arms and planted a kiss on her juicy lips. That kiss turned into something X-rated as my dick tapped on her stomach.

"Down, boy." She chuckled, patting my chest before walking inside of my crib.

Zariah loved on our son like I did when I picked him up from Nanna's house. I loved seeing her and our son together. I couldn't have picked a better woman to be the mother of my son. She was so attentive and overprotective of him, just like she was with me.

"Y'all are stayin' over here tonight." I demanded as I put the groceries up.

"Okay," she replied while putting Jeremy into his playpen.

Like the team that we had always been, preparation for dinner went smoothly. In between cooking dinner and having family time, I couldn't stop telling her how much I appreciated her and our son for being in my life. I rained so many kisses on her face until she sternly told me to stop.

After dinner and bathing our son, he was fast asleep. In my eyes, Jeremy was the perfect son. He didn't cry like most babies I had been around, and he didn't wake up several times throughout the night. The final feeding would send him out like a light. Since he had been on his earth, chunky boy would be sleep around eight forty-five p.m.

Zariah yawned and glared into my face.

"That baby tired?" I questioned as I stood.

"Something like that."

"A'ight. I have just the remedy to make sure that baby sleep good tonight," I voiced with a raised eyebrow.

Laughing, she said, "Look at my Grinch in shiny armor."

Bowing, I replied, "An' he's at yo' service, right motherfuckin' nih."

"Get yo' ass out of here, Fernando." She laughed.

Strolling towards the bathroom, I had a nice play set up for my woman. That was something I had never been shy to do for her. I took pleasure in catering to Zariah. Not once I had skipped out on showering her with love and pleasing her, and I sure as hell wasn't going to stop.

Arriving in the bathroom, I lit her favorite scented candles, made her bath water just the way she liked it, and added her sweet-smelling bath wash. After I created the bubbles, I called Zariah into the bathroom.

"I'm coming," she spoke, waltzing down the hallway.

"Oou, look at my Zaddy," she cooed, stepping into the bathroom.

"You know the drill," I groaned as I anticipated seeing her beautiful, naked body.

"I do," she replied with a huge grin on her face.

Bending, I untied her shoes followed by removing them and her black socks. Next, I unbuckled her belt and pants. Seductively, I pulled down her pants. I licked my lips at the sight of her fat monkey sitting comfortable in a pair of black boy shorts. With her arms raised, I took off her shirt and bra. I saved her panties for last; I loved seeing her walk around with them on, only. Once she was in front of the tub, I stepped behind her, placed soft kisses on her neck before I slowly took those pretty panties off. After my baby got cozy in the hot, bubbly water, our relaxing adult time took place.

While massaging her body, Zariah talked about what she wanted us to get Jeremy for Christmas. Then, the topic of her nothing ass mother showing up at her job talking about her father, Nathan Price took place.

"That's the real reason why you left work, huh?"

Looking into my eyes, she nodded her head.

"Do you want me to step down on that nigga?"

"Nope. He'll get the hint sooner or later that I don't want anything to do with him," she lovingly sighed as I gave the middle of her back a deep-tissue massage.

"A'ight. He ain't got too many times to pressure you into his life, or I'mma go the fuck off. It's past time fo' me to put that nigga in his place," I told her sternly.

"How was your day?" she quickly asked, changing the subject.

"Good. Productive."

"How did the meeting with Gun'em and Poboy went?"

"My sexy woman ... don't worry 'bout all that," I stated, placing a kiss on her button nose.

"I want to..." she replied before I cut her off by gently placing two fingers inside of her.

"Fernandoo," she cooed as I toyed with her pussy.

"You don't need to worry 'bout the Grinch's business ... just Fernando's," I sexily voiced as she lay back on the tub, limbs shaking.

Cooing and nodding her head, she said, "You kills me with that alter ego shit."

"An' I'mma kill you wit' this sex game, too. Get ready to open wide because Daddy need to get inside of you."

Removing my fingers, I quickly stripped out of my clothes. On the verge of stepping into the tub, the doorbell sounded off. Zariah laughed; I didn't. I was pissed off. Most folks wouldn't attempt to answer the door while partaking in adult activities, but I wouldn't enjoy my time with Zariah if I ignored whoever was at my door.

After I put on my clothes, I zipped towards the front door as the knocks sounded off. Inches away from the door, I asked, "Who is it?"

"Maryann," my auntie softly voiced. It seemed as if she had been crying.

Lord, please don't let her tell me something has happened, I thought as I opened the door to see my auntie with sad eyes and tears running down her pretty, light-skinned face.

"Auntie, what's wrong?" I asked as she stepped into my home.

After I closed the door, she slapped the shit out of me and angrily yet sadly said, "I didn't raise you two to run the damn streets. Your parents are rolling over in their graves at the foolishness you are doing with Colby. I've come to terms with losing my son to these ruthless streets … I will *not* lose you, too. Damn it, I cannot lose the only person that is half of my sister. I just can't."

Chapter Four

Zariah

Sunday, December 2nd

"How are things between you and Colby?" I asked Nene as we placed rose-gold, silver, and gold decorations on her white Christmas tree.

"Honey, I really don't know. I'm so tired of dealing with him until it's unbelievable. Yet, I have no choice but to because we have a son and another baby on the way. I just wish that he got his shit together. He really don't believe that the streets don't love him."

"All I can tell you to do is continue talking to him. You might have to do him like I did Fernando. I meant I wasn't putting up with the streets and him. The late night calls, barely being at home, constant fights from niggas that's hating on him, or dealing with the fact that I might lose him to an ignorant bastard in the streets who want what he has."

"That did work well for you, huh?" she asked, placing a blue ornament on the tall tree.

Nodding my head, I said, "Yes, it did."

"You want to know why it worked so well for you?" she quickly asked before answering her question. "Because Grinch loves you more than life itself. He always has. Colby doesn't have that type of love for me."

Feeling sad about her comment, I knew it was time to change the subject. It was the holiday season, time for happiness and love not depression and no love. Wrapping my arms around Nene's petite frame, I told her that everything would work out for the best. Placing her arms around my waist, she leaned her head on my shoulder and began crying.

It had been a long time since she cried—that hurt type of cry; the kind that your soul needed when you were fed up with the shit that you had been putting up with. There was no doubt in my mind that Nene was ready to kick Colby to the curb for good, but I knew it would be hard for her to cut him loose. Not because he was a father to their son, but because they had been sleeping together for over ten years and been in a relationship for three. They had ties together somewhat like Fernando and me. Nene was and had always been in love with Colby, just like I had been with Fernando.

"What would I do without you?" Nene questioned as she broke our embrace and wiped her face.

"Um, probably would be in a looney bin by now." I joked lightly.

With a serious look on her face, she said, "Thank you for being a good friend to me, Zariah. I would never betray or trade you for anything in the world. You are more than a friend to me ... you are like my sister and I appreciate everything you have and will do for me and Colbon."

"Aww, bitch, you know I hate when you start being mushy and shit. You know I'm a big crybaby," I told her as my eyes began to water.

Ring. Ring. Ring.

"Well, bitch you know I get real emotional when I'm with child, so you better get ready for it." She laughed, walking towards the brown entertainment center to retrieve her phone.

Chuckling at her statement, I resumed to decorating her tree all the while thinking about how Nene and I became friends. During our eighth grade year, Nene moved from Robin Warners, Georgia to Montgomery, Alabama. Her first day was pure hell. Girls talked about her like a dog, even though she was fresh—just like me. They hated on her until she spazzed out.

Nene's first day at a new school in a new state kicked off with her stomping out a well-known messy freak, Maleeka Harriot. Seeing that she was about to kill the girl that hated me because of Fernando, I pulled Nene off her and shoved her down the crowded hall. From that day forward, Nene and I were closer than Siamese twins.

We had so much in common. Nene was an only child who was raised by her grandmother. She was extremely pretty, smart, and didn't take mess from anyone. We had a niche for fashion and design. When we got the hang of how to properly use a sewing machine, it was on. Every chance we got, we babysat for people in our neighborhood to earn money for materials. Once we mastered making clothing, we ventured into printing images on shirts. Granted that we didn't have enough money for a digital heat press machine, we left printing images alone. That was until, Fernando bought us an expensive machine for Christmas during our tenth grade year. That day, I learned that the boy I loved with my whole heart had lied to me about not peddling drugs anymore. Everything changed for Fernando and me. Some days were good while others were not; however, he made it his business to keep that part of his life away from him.

"What's up Zariah? Where's Nene?" Colby asked, stepping through the door.

"Hey, Colby. She's in the back," I told him as we hugged.

"A'ight. You good?"

"Yeah. How about yourself?"

"I'm ... I'm fucked up, truth be told," he confessed, sighing.

I knew what he was talking about. Last night, Auntie Maryann cried in Fernando's arms. She informed us that Colby told her what happened between him and Fernando. She made it her business to tell Fernando that she loved him and didn't want harm coming his way.

"Everything will be okay, Colby. You are safe now. Fernando took care of everything. Now, you need to focus on being a better man for yourself, children, and Nene," I stated sincerely before continuing, "You know we be through each other's relationship because we are family, and it's only fair that I let you know that she's on the brink of ghosting you. Do you remember how I fell in the deep end when Fernando was shot?"

Nodding his head, Colby sadly said, "Yeah."

"Do you remember how you felt when he went through that extensive ten-hour surgery?"

"Yeah."

"Times that feeling by one thousand for Nene. Put yourself in her shoes, Colby. Y'all have history together. A whole family y'all have created. That woman is in love with you, but she will not continue to put up with your shit and she doesn't have to. You are smart as fuck and you can't tell me that you aren't. Keep in mind, you were doing my chemistry homework and you were two grades lower than me. Don't let these streets get you when you are so much more than that," I told him in a sisterly manner.

Nodding his head, he replied, "Zariah, I'm addicted to fast money. I hate to see myself workin' a fawty hour job an' bringin' pennies home. I got fo' mouths to feed. These jobs ain't tryin' to take care of a nigga good."

"You are wrong, Colby. It's your job to manage the money well and invest your money into things that will be beneficial to you and your family's future. The hustle money should've been invested. I'm sure Fernando told you that."

"He did, but I didn't wanna hear that shit."

"That was your fault. You better start listening to him. I'm the one putting him up on game."

"Whenever he ready to forgive me fo' fuckin' up, I'mma reach out to him on that tip."

No, you ain't, I thought as I said, "Okay."

"Well, I'll be over when Zariah and I finish putting up Christmas decorations," Nene spoke casually as she stepped into the front room of her two-bedroom apartment.

"Hey, baby. Can we talk?" Colby softly asked Nene as she put her phone on the entertainment center.

"Yeah," she replied blankly before telling me that she would be back.

"Okay."

The apartment was quiet without Colbon being present. Just in case they started arguing, I decided to turn on the T.V. and hook my phone up to the black auxiliary cord hanging from the bottom of the fifty-two inch Vizio T.V.

In the mood to jam, I put on one of my favorite jamming playlists. Instantly, the beat of Kodak Black, Travis Scott, & Offset's "ZeZe"

blasted from the T.V.'s speaker. It was something about the song
that gave you the feeling that you were on an island. I loved the
Caribbean feeling that they song provided; thus, I swayed my hips
while slapping ornaments on the tree. Jigging to the song, I went
into another world. When I brought myself out of the twilight
zone, the song was ending.

As I skipped towards the radio to restart the song, Nene yelled,
"Don't you play that damn song no mo'!"

Laughing, I loudly replied, "Ain't you busy or something? Damn,
why you way up here."

"Because you have worn that song out. I'm tired of hearing it
now." She laughed as "Nympho" by Yung Bleu blasted from the
speakers.

"Ooou, turn that shit up, bitch!" she excitedly yelled.

"That's Fernando calling me," I said shaking my head with a smile
on my face.

"Ah fuck. When y'all are done chatting will you play that song
please?" she begged. Nene and I were big fans of Yung Bleu. How
many times had Fernando and I had gotten really freaky why
listening to his sex songs.

"I sure will," I stated as I ran to my phone, damned near tripping
on the Christmas tree box.

"Fuck!" I loudly said as I answered the phone.

"Yo' sexy ass workin' hard?" Fernando's sexy, deep voice asked.

"Not at all," I replied, cheesing like a schoolgirl.

"That's what's up," he replied while heavily sniffing.

"What are y—"

"Mane, what you don' did in that damn pamper, man? I know damn well you ain't don' … ah hell nawl, Jeremy. Really, fat boy … I mean really," he said in a disgusting tone. Fernando talked to our son as if he could answer him.

Laughing, I asked, "What he did?"

"Shitted every-fuckin'-where. I mean shit is all out the sides of his pamper. It's on the damn covers. Zariah, how am I supposed to clean him wit' all this shit on him?" he asked, gagging.

I couldn't answer right away because of his tone and I could imagine how he was looking. Fernando hated to deal with turds that wasn't his own; yet, he did for our son.

"How bad is it, Fernando?" I asked, chuckling.

"Bad. To the point, I'm finna throw these covers, his clothes, an—"

"Boy, stop playin' in that shit!" Fernando loudly spoke.

"If you don't strip him naked now and put him in the tub. Turn the shower head on and rinse the boo-boo off him. Then, you give him a bath. You better not throw away a single thing, Fernando. Put the covers and his clothes in the washer machine."

He didn't respond because he was too busy gagging and trying to talk shit. I laughed until my stomach hurt.

"What's so funny?" Nene asked as her and Colby stepped into the front room.

"Jeremy shitted out of his pamper and Fernando about to have a heart attack." I laughed.

"Welcome to fatherhood," Colby stated, snickering.

"Zariah, baby, please come home an' help me. I can't deal wit' this stench. The sight of baby shit is doin' somethin' to me. I promise you I will compensate you fo' leavin'." He sweetly begged.

"I'm not leavin', Fernando. You got this baby. It's just baby shi—"

"Jeremy, stop kickin' yo' legs ... you spreadin' the funk an' little chunks of shit 'round. Son, I really need you to work wit' me," Fernando sighed as I heard the shower being turned on.

"Let me go over there an' help this sad ass nigga out," Colby said as I doubled over in laughter at my son's father.

Before he left, Colby passionately kissed Nene and told her that he loved her.

"Love you too."

I stayed on the phone coaching Fernando on how to get rid of the shit smell. Ten minutes later, I heard Colby's voice as Fernando fought to put on Jeremy's clothes. I was surprised that Fernando willingly let Colby in. That was a good sign; my baby was willing to be in his favorite cousin's presence, once again.

"Well, since Colby is there to assist yo—"

"Oou, Grinch! Mane, what he don' ate?" Colby shrieked in a panicked tone in between gagging.

I pressed the speakerphone icon as Fernando said, "What in the hell? Come on Jeremy. What is wrong wit' yo' guts, mane?"

"Cuz, shit on my pants! I thought he was don'. What did he eat? What did he eat?" Colby voiced as they gagged.

"Zariah, baby please comes home," Fernando stated in a defeated tone as Nene and I were in tears.

"Okay. I'm on the way," I told him as I disconnected my phone and placed my boots on my feet. Nene slipped on her shoes and grabbed her jacket.

As we made our way to my car, Colby asked Fernando what he fed Jeremy.

"Eggs, grits, bread, an' applesauce."

I was weak to my stomach as my vision became blurry because I was laughing so hard. Fernando was the reason why Jeremy's bowels were disturbed. Our son loved applesauce, but it didn't agree with him.

Hopping in the front seat, trying to control my laughter, I said, "Fernando, you must have been watching the sports channel?"

"Yeah," he replied as I heard water running.

"Go figures. I been told you to stop feeding him applesauce because it messes with his tummy really bad."

"Ah, fuck. How long he gonna be shitty?"

"Depends on how much you gave him."

"Hell, we had fo' cups."

Shaking my head, I said, "Well, he will be shitting for a while. I'm on the way now."

"Okay. Thank you, baby. I owe you big time."

"An' y'all asses owe me!" Colby voiced.

Ending the call, I laughed at the foolishness we were going to witness, shortly.

Getting serious, Nene looked at me and said, "Colby will be looking for a job in the morning. He promised me that he would leave the streets alone and make things right for himself and our future."

"It sounds like you don't believe him."

"I don't. I've heard that shit before. One too many times type of before."

"This is a tough conversation to have since I've been in your shoes before, and honestly I'm back in them since the deal that was made between Poboy and Fernando. So, I'm a little on edge as well. All I can do is trust what Fernando says, but if things go back to the way they were Jeremy and I are gone and we ain't coming back."

"I'm sorry that Colby put y'all in this situation. I really am. You already know I cussed his ass out bad about that."

Giggling, I said, "If I don't know anything, I know you gave that nigga a run for his money with that mouthpiece of yours."

Ring. Ring. Ring.

Expecting it to be Fernando, I quickly answered my phone. I was highly disappointed as I heard my mother's voice.

"What's up, girl? What are you doin'?" she asked as if she was a young chick.

Rolling my eyes, I sighed, "What do you want, Patricia?"

Since I had been on this earth, I have never called her Momma and she didn't correct me. She wasn't a parent, more of an associate. Even thought, she didn't deserve to be called Momma, I wasn't disrespectful towards her.

"To see can I make som' extra money by watchin' Jeremy," she replied, popping gum.

"I don't have anything planned."

"Well, you need to plan something with Grinch, so I can make the money to buy me an outfit or at least a new wig." She confessed while exhaling.

With an odd facial expression, I asked, "Why Nathan ain't give you any money, Patricia?"

"Because his new bitch told him he need to stop doing fo' me."

Shaking my head at the pathetic woman that gave birth to me, I quickly said, "Well, go get a job. That's what most people of working age do. They work to take care of themselves."

"No, ma'am. I've never had a job, and I sure as hell ain't going to get one now. Chile, I'm too beautiful to work on any man's job and that's facts."

"And look where that 'beautiful' look has gotten you. Nowhere," I stated in a matter-of-fact tone as I pulled into Fernando's driveway.

"Anyways, girl. Yo' father wants you and Jeremy to come to his house next Saturday. He's having a cookout and wants you to become close with your siblings and him."

"If you don't get off my phone with that mess. Like I told him, I don't want a relationship with him or his kids. I'm fine. I don't want them in my life at all. All they know is being criminals and getting over on people. I'm good with my circle."

"Oh, so it's true … you do think you are too good to be around people that share the same blood, huh?" she asked, laughing.

Growing angry with the stupid woman, I nastily replied, "Precisely. I'm too good to be around people who will only try to find a way to fuck up my life. I'm good on that front. You should be to good to be around them as well. The same people that have *never* gave a single care about your well-being. Blood don't mean anything to them as it doesn't to you. In case you forgot, you chose a kingpin over me. The same kingpin that blessed you with me. So, you can get off my phone with that nonsense. Tell Nathan I said go to hell, and if you keep on trying to pressure me into acknowledging him … you can follow him."

Ending the call, I asked God to forgive me for being disrespectful towards Patricia. Afterwards, I performed breathing exercises before stepping out of my car. The last thing I needed was for Fernando to find out that Patricia was harassing me to spend time with Nathan and his children.

"Is having Nathan and his children in your life that stressful?" Nene inquired as we stepped out of the car.

"More than you would ever know," I told her as we closed the doors.

So stressful to the point I'm ready to put a restraining order on all of their asses.

Chapter Five

Grinch

I was so glad to see Zariah stroll her beautiful self into my room with Nene behind her. While Nene and I greeted each other, Zariah stepped in and took charge like the boss she was to her family of three.

"Good jump on messing with Daddy, Jeremy," Zariah babbled in baby talk.

After smacking her on the ass, I skipped out of the bathroom to start the washing machine. Colby did me a solid by putting the bed clothes along with his jeans in the cleaning machine. I thought I was going to pass out from the sight of my son's shit spread across the sheets. The stench was enough to make me mad for forgetting that his little guts couldn't take applesauce.

"Aye, can we have a man-to-man talk?" Colby asked from the kitchen, pouring him a cup of orange Kool-Aid.

"Yeah," I told him as I poured two cups of laundry detergent on top of the pile of clothes.

Walking away from the black washing machine, Colby made his way towards my man cave. Once inside, I closed the door behind me as I fired up a cigarette and placed a towel behind the door. I was sure that Zariah, Nene, and Jeremy would chill out in the front room. I was big on Jeremy not smelling any type of smoke.

Flipping on the T.V. and the gaming system, Colby asked, "Do you think I would be great on someone's job?"

"Yep."

"What do you think I'm good at doin'?"

"Anything, honestly. You ain't no dumb nigga, Colby. It won't take you long to catch on to any position within a job. You just have to apply yo'self."

"Do you think I can work at International Papers wit' you?"

"Hell, yes. I need a member on my team. We are short two people, so the overtime hours is bananas right now. I had to take this weekend off to spend wit' them before I pull close to seventy hours a week."

"Can I use yo' computer to fill out the application?"

"You better not ask that dumb ass question no mo' nigga." I shot back with a raised eyebrow.

Chuckling while taking a seat, Colby flipped open my laptop and began typing. As I glared at him, I wondered whether he was serious about getting a job. There has been plenty of times he filled out job applications, had an interview scheduled, and didn't go to the interview. The last thing I needed was for him to get in the door and shame me.

"Are you going to stick wit' the job if you are hired?"

"Hell yes. The look in Momma an' Nene's eyes yesterday an' this mawnin' put a nigga in a bad spot. If I fail, then my son fail, an' that's not what I want. Yeah, I love fast money, but I love them mo'," he genuinely voiced while looking at me.

Sighing heavily as I put the cigarette out, I asked, "What made you come clean to Auntie?"

"I walked into the kitchen to a conversation that I wished I had not. Momma had asked Colbon what he wanted to be when he grew up and his response shook the shit out of me. He said that wanted to run the streets like his daddy an' get fast money."

With a wow'ed facial expression, I stared at Colby.

"He see the money, an' me gettin' him an' his momma everything they want, but he doesn't know 'bout the underdog shit that goes on. Right then, I knew I had to change fo' him. Even if Nene was to take him away from me, he would still want to be a street runner because he's seen me doin' it."

"Auntie came by here last night an' fired my face the fuck up."

"I kinda figured that's where she went after cussin' me out an' puttin' som' knots on the back of my head."

"Apparently, Uncle Colby wasn't there."

"Hell nawl, if he was my ass would be dead ret nih," he voiced seriously.

"Do you think Auntie gonna tell him?"

"No."

"An' you really believe that?"

"I made her a deal that she couldn't refuse."

"Colby, do you know what Auntie said to me when she fired my ass up?"

As he shook his head, I made sure to tell him his mother's behavior and the words she cried to me as I held her in my arms.

Dropping his head, Colby voice, "She doesn't believe me."

"Nope, an' do you blame her, Colby?"

"We got caught in som' fucked up situation fo' no reason. We was thuggin' fo' no damn reason. I came wit' money an' som' coins ducked off fo' me when I turned twenty-one. I didn't have no business sellin' drugs because the niggas that we hung out wit' did."

While chatting about our growing up days and the nonsense that we did, Colby filled out the application for my job and many others. I couldn't lie as if I didn't feel like Auntie. Colby was more in tune with selling drugs and getting fast money versus to doing things the right way. I knew it was going to be a matter of time before he proved Auntie and me wrong. Yeah, I wanted the best for him, but he was highly unlikely to do right.

Ring. Ring. Ring.

Pulling my phone out of my jogging pants, I saw Gun'em's name. Quickly, I answered.

"What's up, fool?"

"Coolin'. I'm outside."

"Come in."

"I need to holla at cha. Come outside fo' a minute," he replied, exhaling.

"Bet," I replied as I hopped to my feet and ended the call.

Walking out of my man cave, the T.V. was on a cooking channel as the ladies placed a glass filled with a golden liquid to their lips. I didn't see Fat Daddy amongst them; I knew that he was asleep. I had to address what was in their glasses. One thing I didn't like was a woman drinking while pregnant. That shit did something to me.

"Nene, I know you ain't drinkin', guh?" I asked in a strong pastor voice.

"No. It's apple juice, Pastor Grinch," she replied, causing Zariah to giggle.

"Okay. Zariah?"

"Yeah?"

After licking my lips, I seductively said, "You ain't pregnant yet, so you gettin' right fo' me?"

"Get on somewhere, Fernando." She snickered.

"Oh, so you finally took his ass off condom probation."

"Mind your damn business," my lady spoke while laughing.

"I'm finna step outside an' holla at Gun'em fo' a minute," I told Zariah before they started to talk mad shit.

"Okay. Tell him hey an' congratulations on the new baby with Trina."

As I nodded my head, Nene loudly spat, "What!"

Quickly placing her hand over her mouth, I laughed and opened the door.

"Chile, my poor co-worker so distraught about being pregnant until it's not funny," Zariah voiced as I closed the door behind me.

Skipping down the steps, I could not wait to tell Gun'em what Zariah had said to Nene. I hoped that would help him with winning over his little broad.

"What's up, nigga?" we stated to each other while dapping.

"Aye, before we discuss business, I need to tell you that yo' guh still distraught 'bout being pregnant. If you need help gettin' good wit' yo' chick, you might want to chop it up wit' Zariah."

With a frown on his face, I did not give him a chance to ask any questions. I delivered answers to him.

"I hate to say this, but um, our business can wait. I need to chat wit' Zariah about Trina fo' a minute if you don't mind," he voiced, hopping out of the driver's seat.

"Nih, nigga, you know I don't mind. Shid, this is an important matter, so handle yo' business."

The moment he stepped inside, he greeted the women and began talking to my gorgeous woman. She told him how Trina acted at work and what her thinking process was like. The look on

Gun'em's face made me feel sad. I knew without a doubt that he was eager to be a father. Gun'em was the type of dude that was extremely careful in the sex department. If he didn't see a future with a broad, he didn't sleep with her unprotected.

"Zariah, what do I do? She's the only one a nigga been fuckin' wit' fo' two years. I cut the other chickens off because I saw a future wit' her. I don' said everything that I needed to say to keep her on board, an' to let her know that I ain't goin' nowhere. I went as far as to propose to her. She shot me down so quick … damn near had a nigga in tears."

With a wicked smile on her face, Zariah looked at Nene and asked, "Would you like me to cook your favorite food tonight?"

"Oou, bitch … girl time wit' a splash of no manners niggas in the house an' a shitty booty little baby."

Nene laughed as Colby stepped into the hallway.

"What y'all don' cooked up nih?" Colby asked, walking into the living room and dapping up Gun'em.

"I'm havin' woman problems an' they gonna help a nigga out," Gun'em stated as Zariah's phone rang.

"Speaking of the devil," she said while looking at Gun'em.

"That's dat baby?" he questioned with a smile on his face.

"Yep," she replied, answering the phone.

The room became quiet as we listened to the conversation between Trina and Zariah. My baby was a natural at calming people. Her soothing, soft voice would make the devil's soul get right.

"I'm cooking dinner tonight if you would like to come over and hang out with my friend Nene and me," Zariah said as she looked at Gun'em whom was sitting on the edge of the sofa.

Once Zariah nodded her head at Gun'em, she asked Trina, "Is seven o'clock good?"

Apparently, Trina said yes because Zariah gave her my address. Gun'em's facial expression informed us that he was pleased with Zariah's attempt to getting him back in the good graces of his pregnant chick.

"Yeah, you are more than welcome to come over now that way you and Nene can vibe."

"Alright. I'll see you soon," she stated before saying bye and ending the call.

"Thank you, Zariah," Gun'em voiced, sincerely.

"Don't thank me yet. My job is far from done," she replied before sipping from the half-empty glass.

Clearing my throat before his chick showed up, I stood and said, "Now, to our business."

"Yeah, let's do that."

"You might want to put your truck in the garage," Zariah stated to Gun'em.

"Nawl, he ain't gotta do that. Once we come back inside, we'll be in the man cave. All you gotta do is tell her that he left out wit' me, Colby, an' Uncle Colby."

Once we had the set up in play, Gun'em and I stepped onto the porch. He told me that we had approximately ten minutes before she pulled up, if she was leaving from her apartment. Without further ado, we got down to business. In one minute, I learned that our original play of setting Poboy up with a bunch of bad bitches was useless. Gun'em told me that he received word that Poboy was bisexual and that he had a nigga that he dealt with during the night—in a different city, so that no one would find out.

"Is he in love wit' the nigga?" I asked with my hands on top of my head.

"My sources told me that he is. He's waitin' 'til he put the streets on lock before comin' out the closet."

"Do you have the dude's information?"

"You know I do, an' you'll be surprised to know who it is."

Dropping my hand from my head, I asked, "Who is it?"

"Zariah's uncle ... Tremaine Price."

With bucked eyes, I lowly replied, "No-motherfuckin'-way."

Laughing, my partner in crime said, "Oh, yes-motherfuckin'-way. No better way to skin a cat."

With a wicked smile on my face, I said, "Woe, this shit is going to be too easy. The moment Poboy learns that Tremaine snitched on him, they will have it out."

"Yep, an' I already set that shit in motion. All we gotta do is make sure the bond between them are weak as fuck."

"How we do that?"

"You know I got a criminally gay uncle, right?"

"Yeah."

"Well, I was askin' him a bunch of questions that would help us further bury that nigga an' those 'round him."

"Are the other niggas fruity?"

"Nope. The plan still goes fo' them."

"A'ight," I quickly replied before saying, "Shouldn't we be going inside of the house now?"

"Yep."

Stepping into the crib, Colby was sitting on the sofa looking like a sad puppy. There was never a time when I didn't incorporate him in my business, but this time I couldn't. I was afraid that he would fuck this up and I couldn't have that.

"Aye, Colby, we finna hit the man-cave up. Ready to get yo' ass whooped in a game or two?" I asked as Gun'em said how much he was betting on the game.

With an attitude, Colby said, "Nawl, I'm good. I'm finna head out."

"You finna go home?" Nene inquired.

"Why does it matter where I go? You ain't tryin' to hear shit I got to say." He shot back, standing.

"You put a strain on us. Don't get mad at me. Yeah, we discussed things at my apartment. However, you gotta show me you are ready to change. Your words don't mean shit to me anymore. Only actions, Colby."

"I'mma holla at y'all later," he said before exiting my crib.

An eerie silence overtook my home. As we looked at one another with a blank facial expression, I shook my head and said, "Lord, please don't let me have to bury my cousin. I got a feelin' he finna do som' stupid shit."

Chapter Six

Zariah

Wednesday, December 5th

After the talk Nene and I had with Trina, my mind had not been the same. I tried my best not to think of the things that could go wrong as Fernando jumped back into a dangerous part of the streets—conspiring with Nene's dumb ass cousins, Poboy and his crew. Those niggas were not the type of people that could be trusted. People with common sense would run the moment they saw them coming. With a snap of their fingers, a shootout would take place just as quickly as a fight between two females that had been arguing about which one was the better side bitch to a nothing ass guy.

"Hey, are you okay?" Trina's soft voice spoke.

"Yes, I am. Why do you ask?" I inquired while stocking several new model Dell laptops into the correct bins underneath the display laptop.

"You have been extremely quiet today."

"Just have a lot on my mind." I smiled politely.

"Would it be about the same thing that I'm going through?"

"Not really, but sort of," I sighed, moving loose strands of hair away from my face.

"Well, I see that your mind is still boggled. Whenever you want to talk, I'm here for you."

Pleasantly, I smiled and said thank you.

Throughout my shift, I had remained silent and completed tasks for next week with minimal speaking to any of the employees underneath me. My superiors questioned me on what had me quiet. Being the private person that I was, I simply told them that today was just a quiet day for me. I didn't like the way that I felt, and I had to inform Fernando of my feelings.

Close towards the end of my shift, my boss stepped to me and said, "You have a call on line three."

Nodding my head, I replied, "Okay."

My nerves didn't sit well with me; I rarely received a call at my job. If someone needed me, they knew to call my cell phone. Upon reaching the black, professional phone, my shaky hand lifted it out of the cradle and pressed the slender button beside the number three.

"Hello, this is Zariah," I professionally stated as calm as I could.

"So, you think you are too good to be in my presence?" Nathan questioned, chuckling.

Anger consumed me immediately. Who in the fuck did he think he was calling me at my place of employment?

"First of all, yes I do think that I'm too good to be in your presence. Why are you running behind someone who hates that you exist?"

"I want to have a bond wit' you, MaZariah."

"Not the type of bond that a father should have with his children. All of your kids are corrupt, and I'm not up for that life. Why don't you harass them? Aren't they doing everything that you ask of them? Why meddle with an individual like myself?"

"Look, I thought I made myself clear to your uppity ass that I wanted you up front and center this weekend so that you can get to know your family."

"And I swore I have told you and your piece of shit of family that I don't want anything to do with y'all. Contact me again, and I will make sure that your little empire will crumble, Nathan Price. I've saved your ass one time before. I will not do it again, and I mean it. Leave me the fuck alone," I nastily stated through clenched teeth.

"Listen here, little bitch, you are yo' mother's child. You will do as I say, just like she do. If I want you to sell yo' lil' pussy, you will do that. If I want you to have mo' children, I control that. Don't get it twisted like I can't make yo' life a livin' hell because I can. That *boyfriend* of yo's would disappear within a blink of an eye, an' it would be all because of me. You ain't shit but the sperm that I didn't let yo' mother swallow," he snarled.

For Nathan to talk to me as if I was the dirt on the soles of his shoes brought tears to my eyes. Clutching my chest, I held onto the phone with nothing to say. I had never been spoken to in such a manner that made me feel as if I was a waste of space. If I hadn't hated him for not allowing my mother to properly care for me, I sure as hell hated him now. If I hadn't hated him for putting drugs in my book bag at the age of five and sending me on my way to school, I really hated that bastard now as I held tightly onto the phone.

As he continued talking to me disrespectfully, I finally found the will to say, "Count your days bitch because they are coming."

After hanging up the phone and drying my eyes, I realized it was time for me to clock out. Walking towards the back, a couple of customers tried stopping me, but I directed them to the nearest worker on the floor. I was not able to communicate with anyone after the call with the man that helped my mother create me.

From the time I reached the clock-out station until I arrived home with my son, my mind was not in the proper place. It seemed as things went in a blur as I rehashed the hurtful words and tone that Nathan spoke to me. He was out to get me because I didn't want to be a part of his criminal ways. I wasn't a horrible person because I didn't want to be associated with that lifestyle. Yet, he, my mother, and his family made me feel that way.

"Zariah!" Fernando yelled as I quickly wiped my face and looked at Jeremy playing with his pacifier.

"Yeah," I replied as I kicked off my shoes.

"Why haven't you answered my calls or texts?" he asked while strolling towards my room.

"I didn't hear my phone. It's still on vibrate," I told him as he graced me with a worried expression plastered on his handsome face.

"What's wrong wit' you?" he inquired as Jeremy began his babbling.

"Nothing," I lied while glaring into his face.

"One thing you can't do is lie to me, Zariah. So, I'mma ask you again … what's wrong wit' you?" he asked, taking a seat next to me on the bed.

"Just been a long day and I'm tired. Shouldn't you be sleep for work tonight?"

"Yeah, but you know I call an' make sure that you an' Jeremy arrived home safely before goin' to sleep. When you didn't answer my ten calls or five texts, I came over to see what's up," he stated while connecting our hands together.

Sighing heavily while rolling my neck from side-to-side, Fernando kissed my neck while massaging my hand. Relaxing at the firmness of his hand and the softness of his lips, I softly whimpered.

"Go relax in the shower, I'll cuddle up wit' big guy. Wash yo' stressful day away," he sweetly whispered in my ear.

The things that he said and his actions were the reasons why I loved him so much. He was not a selfish person, never had been. Caring, loving, thoughtful, and overprotective were the reasons why I always second guessed leaving him for his dabbling in the streets. Fernando was every woman's dream man; a man that would provide through rain, sleet, hail, and snow; the type of man that you would drop on one knee and ask his ass to marry you.

"Okay," I replied as I planted a delicate kiss on his soft lips.

As I stepped away from my bed, Fernando began playing and talking to our son. The little laughs that escaped Jeremy's mouth were breathtaking. I lived to see my son's behavior towards his father. Before partaking in a much-needed hot shower, I watched the two interact as if they hadn't seen each other in a long time.

With a smile on my face, I skipped to the bathroom. Turning on the water knobs, the unwanted conversation between Nathan and I reappeared. I tried looking in the mirror and saying positive things that would make the memory go away, but it didn't work. I left the mirror with my hand clasped over my mouth as I silently cried. While crying, I wondered why Nathan had to say those hurtful things to me. What kind of man would speak to his daughter in that manner? Not one that truly cared for the creation that he helped make.

While I cried, I prayed that Fernando wouldn't come into the bathroom. My prayer went unanswered as the door opened. The look on my man's face was enough to make me melt into the ground. Quickly, I wiped my face and tried to get myself together.

"You promised to never keep anythin' from me; yet, you are in the bathroom cryin'. What is wrong, Zariah? Are you worried 'bout me? Are you thinkin' 'bout leavin' me because I have to work wit' Poboy an' nem?"

That was an issue, but it wasn't the reason I was crying. Fernando didn't need to know the real reason; thus, I nodded my head. Scooping me into his arms, he rained kisses on my forehead and lips while holding me tightly.

"I need you to believe me when I say that I'm goin' to be fine. Gotta work out som' kinks an' I will be as free as you have wished fo' me to be. There is nothin' in this world that will take me away from you an' our son, an' I mean that shit. Okay?"

Slowly nodding my head as I gazed into his eyes, I softly replied, "Okay."

"Hurry up an' take a shower. I wanna lay wit' you an' Jeremy before I have to leave fo' work."

"Okay."

Doing as my man said, I cleaned my body. Feeling the hot water beating on my temple, I closed my eyes and performed breathing exercises. Afterwards, I deeply inhaled the flowery-scented body wash that lathered perfectly into my pink loofah. While rinsing off my body, my mind was on the two people lying in my bed. A loving smile crept on my face as I ensured that my body was free of soap. Pleased with a water-beaded body, I turned off the water and escaped the tub with a big, light-green towel wrapped around my body.

"I love it when you step out of the bathroom wit' only a towel on. I think it's time fo' me to put chunky boy in his room, an' love on his momma," Fernando sexily growled while picking up our son and slowly walking towards me.

"After the type of day that I had, Momma needs Daddy to put her mind at ease," I seductively spat as I dropped the towel at the foot of the bed.

"An' I'm promise you Daddy gonna ease yo' mind oh so well," he whispered in my ear before licking my earlobe.

When Fernando's sexy self returned, he delivered his promise so great that I begged him to call in from work. My pleas went unanswered when he kissed the top of my forehead and said, "Daddy gotta work to care fo' y'all. So, I gotta hit that clock, baby."

"Ughh," I sighed as I twist and turned in the bed.

Chuckling as he moved towards the bathroom, he said, "I'll get you right when you get off work tomorrow. You know this."

"Okay," I yawned, eyelids heavy.

Looking at the clock on the DVR box, it read six thirty. It was to early to go to sleep, but I didn't care. My mental stated was exhausted more so than my body. By the time Fernando turned on the shower, my eyelids were closed as my body relaxed.

I was slightly awakened by him whispering in my ear, "Before I leave, I'll give Jeremy a wash off an' place him in the bed wit' you. When I get to work, I'll call you. I love you, Zariah."

"Be safe and I love you, Fernando," I sleepily replied, pulling him closer to me so that we could engage in a passionate kiss that would surely send me to bed feeling wonderful.

Chapter Seven

Grinch

"You think you gonna raise taxes on me, Poboy?" a slim nigga in the break room asked in a low tone while standing in front of the vending machine.

Now, this is a conversation worth hearin', I thought as I placed my wireless Bluetooth in my ear as I pulled out two dollars for snacks.

Bobbing my head and jigging to nothing, I had to pretend that I wasn't paying attention to the dude. Just like the dummy I thought he would be, the nigga kept talking.

"Raise them taxes if you wanna an' see what the fuck really gonna happen to you. I got pictures of you an' that nigga Tremaine. I promise you everyone in the world gonna know what you like to do in yo' spare time. Wanna reconsider now?"

I need that damn phone.

Shortly afterwards, slim dude chuckled before saying, "I thought you might reconsider. Have a good night."

Still in mode as if I was listening to music, I snatched my snacks out of the vending machine all the while with a smile on my face. Once I was out of the break room, I walked outside to the smoking area and dialed Gun'em's number. I was glad that I was the only one outside. I knew that wouldn't last long, so I prayed that

Gun'em answered before I didn't have the opportunity to say anything.

My prayers went answered on the second ring.

When my partner's deep voice answered, he happily greeted, "What's up hardworkin' nigga?"

I didn't have time to joke with the nigga since I was calling with an urgent message.

"Aye, I need you to be up at this job 'round midnight. I'm goin' to send you a picture of a dude an' I need you to get his phone," I quickly said.

"A'ight. If he don't come out 'round that time, is it wise fo' me to wait 'til y'all shift end?"

With a smile on my face, I replied, "An' you fuckin' know it. We need that phone. It'll make our plans just that sweeter. Feel me?"

Evilly laughing, Gun'em asked, "Don't tell me that a nut at yo' job got photos of Poboy an' Tremaine together?"

"An' you fuckin' know it," I stated as the slim dude stepped outside on the phone.

Being the slick nigga that I was, I began talking as if I was on the phone with a broad. Thus, making Gun'em say, "Nigga, that's why I fucks wit' you. You be on som' illy shit. You don't mind takin' photos of a bih."

"Shid, guh, you know I be down fo' whatever. So, whatcha really talkin' 'bout? Show me som' titties before I start workin'," I spoke casually as I took several pictures of the dude.

Gun'em laughed as I took plenty of pictures, so that he wouldn't mistake the nigga for anyone else. Continuing with my slick talk, I sent the photos to Gun'em.

In a matter of seconds, he said, "A'ight, I'll handle my end."

"A'ight. I'll see you when a nigga get off," I replied, standing.

"Bet."

Walking towards the door, I placed my phone on vibrate and smiled. Stepping into the building, I couldn't wait until midnight. I would be one-step closer to deadening the Forge boys. Zariah and I would continue living peacefully with our son, just the way we intended.

"What up, Grinch?" two of my employees stated while moving towards our department.

"Shit, ready to get these hours over wit'," I told them as we entered our working area.

For our shift to run smoothly, I had a set amount of things that I needed to do before my crew began working. As three inspectors checked forklifts and other devices that we needed to load products into trucks, I checked the logs to see how many trucks were on the yard and how many were due for the duration of our work hours.

With a raised eyebrow, I threw my head back and sighed heavily. According to the logs, we were going to have a long, productive night. Clearing my throat, I called for my team's attention. Like always, they gave me their undivided attention as I glared into each of their faces.

"Alright, ladies an' gents. We will have a full night ahead of us. We will take the designated breaks an' nothin' mo'. Keep in mind that if we run a great percentage as a whole, we bring in som' good money fo' next week's paycheck. Like always, we work as a team while being safe an' on that note let's get this money," I told them, ending my prep talk.

The first two hours went great, and I had a good rhythm going as I loaded trucks along with my crew. I loved working with the diverse individuals; they knew how to handle pressure. I couldn't have asked to be a supervisor of a better team. Our shift was known for winning contests and other incentives that the company bestowed upon us.

Through my several layers of clothing, I felt my cell phone vibrating. I wasn't in a position to check it since I was loading a truck. By the seventh vibration, I knew the call was an eager matter; thus, I finished loading the truck before slipping away to check my phone. At the sight of seeing Nene's and Zariah's names, my heart raced as I dialed Zariah's number. She didn't answer the phone, so I called Nene.

"Hello," she said, calmly.

"What's wrong, Nene?"

"Nothing, well, I don't know if everything is okay or not. Grinch, have you talked to Colby?"

"No, why?"

"I haven't talked to him since the day we were at your house. Grinch, I'm worried about him," she softly replied.

"You know how he do, Nene. He stay gone fo' a minute then pop back up on the scene like he ain't disappeared."

"That is true, but even if he's mad at me, he will still call and talk to Colbon."

With a frown on my face, I asked, "Wait, he hasn't called Colbon … at all?"

"No. That's why I'm so worried about him. He never missed one night without telling our son that he loves him."

Now, I was worried. It wasn't like Colby to not call his son. My cousin was many things, but a deadbeat dad was not one of them. Ending the call with Nene, I dialed Colby's number. The call went to voicemail; I called three more times before sighing heavily and walking back into my working area.

An hour later, I couldn't perform well. Colby was on my mind. Not wanting to, I knew that I had to find my cousin. Going to my boss, I told him that I had a family emergency. The second he granted me to leave, I flew out of the business with thoughts of where Colby could be. As I hopped in my vehicle, I tried calling him again.

"Shit, woe, answer the damn phone," I growled, feeling my temperature rise.

One thing I knew, he better not be doing anything stupid that would result in me putting a bullet in his ass or someone else. As I zoomed away from the parking lot, I called Gun'em.

"What's up, woe?"

"Aye, have you seen Colby?"

"Nawl. Why?"

"He ain't answerin' the phone."

Chuckling, he replied, "The nigga probably laid up wit' a bitch or som'. Nigga felt a lil' salty the other day, so you know how yo' cousin do when he get in that fuck-boy phase."

"He ain't called Colbon since that day," I told him as I turned on the main road that would lead me to Montgomery.

"Oh, shit. You need me to put out word on that nigga?"

"Yeah."

"Do you still want me to come up to the job?"

"Hell yeah. I need you in that joint, but I ain't there. Tell the guards that you are there to surprise yo' girlfriend Lisa Monroe wit' breakfast. Make sure yo' ass bring food, nigga."

"Bet, but um who is Lisa Monroe?" he inquired, curiously.

"Mane, don't worry 'bout all that. That's a fo' sho way fo' you to get in without any hassles."

"Oh, she a head bitch in charge, huh?"

"Yeah," I replied with a smile on my face.

"A'ight. I'll call you once I leave wit' the phone."

"Okay, an' let me the second you get word on where Colby at."

"Bet."

When the call ended, I laughed and said, "That nigga gonna be at my ass when he leave the job."

Lisa Monroe was far from the head bitch in charge. Lisa was in the process of undergoing a sex change. She was turning that ding-a-ling into a coochie. Little buds on her chest had formed six months ago. Gun'em was surely going to try to tear the top out off my head if he stepped to Lisa and realized what she was.

While aiming for Colby's home, my cell phone rang. By the loving ringtone, I knew it was Auntie Maryann. Quickly, I answered the phone.

"Hello," I said.

"Fernando," Uncle Colby stated in his deep baritone voice.

"Sir?"

"Have you talked to Colby?"

"Not since the other day, Unc. What's up?"

"Your auntie and I have been trying to call him for two days with no luck. Nene just left here looking for him. We went to his house, and he wasn't there. Do you have any idea where he at?" he asked in a worried tone.

"No, sir."

"Is he in any trouble?"

"No, sir."

"Then why wouldn't he answer any of our calls?"

Sighing heavily, I replied, "Now, that I can't answer. I got off to see what's up wit' him. Once I find him, I'll call an' let you know."

Before my uncle could say anything, Auntie Maryann blurted out, "He probably in the streets doing something he has no business doing. I'm telling you now, I'm done with my son. He ain't going to do right. We didn't raise him to be selling drugs and carrying on like he ain't got good sense. Now, he finna drag Fernando back into this shit. I'm sick of Colby ... just plain damn sick of his ass."

I prayed that Auntie Maryann was wrong. I hoped the talk that Colby and I had didn't go down the drain. I needed him to do right so that I could. I badly wanted him to get his head on straight so that he could provide the best for his family.

"I will call y'all back," I stated as I pulled into the quiet trailer home community that Colby lived in, eight minutes away from my job.

"Okay," they replied before sighing.

Pulling into the double parking spot in front of Colby's nice, doublewide trailer, I laughed as I saw his poor attempt at hiding his car behind my Escalade truck. Shutting off the engine, I stepped into the brisk air and walked towards the front door.

I knocked four times before using the backup key to enter his living quarters. Low and behold, he was on the sofa. Colby was loudly snoring while the T.V. was on Cartoon Network. Closing and locking the door, I called out to him. He didn't stir as he was snuggled underneath a thick, white cover.

"Colby!" I yelled, walking closer to him.

"Huh?" he asked loudly and oddly while looking around with big, moist eyes.

"Dude, you got folks callin' an' lookin' fo' yo' ass. You ain't heard yo' phone ringin', knocks at the door, or the doorbell sounding off?" I asked as he drew up his legs and closed his eyes.

"Nawl, fuckin' head an' back killin' me. Took som' over-the-counter pain pills fo' this horrible ass headache. What's up?" he asked, running his hand down his face.

"Them migraines back?"

"In full fuckin' force. Them hoes ain't lettin' up on my ass."

"How long they been kickin' yo' ass?"

"'Bout two weeks nih."

"You been to the doctor?"

"Yeah, an' gotta see another one tomorrow."

"A'ight."

Colby had been dealing with migraine issues since he was ten. There were plenty of times our room was darker than a cave, which used to scare the hell out of me.

"I wished yo' ass would've told us that the demon was back to hauntin' you. A nigga had to get off work to find yo' ass," I said in a casual tone.

"Well, now you see that I ain't in no shit, you can go back to work. A nigga gucci. Just been sleep."

Hearing the unpleasant tone, I chuckled and asked, "Why you ain't talked to Nene or Colbon since you left my crib, woe?"

"She got a nigga in the friend zone, so I don't have a reason to call her phone."

"Dude, y'all got a son together."

"An' what the fuck does that supposed to mean?" he asked, sitting up and glaring into my face.

"That you need to reach out to him like you been doin'."

"An' who in the fuck said I hadn't been reachin' out to my boy?"

"You ain't called Nene's phone since the day you left my crib, bruh."

Chuckling, he replied, "Y'all really think I'm that damn stupid, huh? Fo' you an' everybody else fuckin' info, when I left yo' crib an' shit I went an' bought my boy a phone so I wouldn't have to call Nene's phone. She don't want nothin' to do wit' me, so ain't no need in me hittin' her line to talk to Colbon. He can tell me himself what he need. When it comes down to the baby, if she decides to keep it, I'm sure she'll send a text or som' shit."

With a curious facial expression, I asked, "So, you been talkin' to Colbon?"

"Yeah, I talked to him before that medicine got ahold of my ass."

"Nih, I don' got off work because I thought somethin' don' happened to yo' ass. You got everybody thinkin' somethin' wrong, an' yo' ass laid up in this bitch sleepin' an' soundin' like a fuckin' bear. Mane, let me call these folks of ours an' let them know you good."

"If they were smart enough, they would've saw my poor attempt of hidin' my car behind yo' truck." He laughed.

"Speakin' of that … what in the fuck yo?" I questioned, laughing with my phone in my hand.

"Mane, that Excedrin P.M. ain't no bullshit. That shit caught me eight minutes after I took the fucka. I swear I couldn't finish puttin' the car cover on the front end. My damn muscles was lettin' me know that they were failin' on me. I'm still drowsy nih. If yo' ass hadn't interrupted my sleep, I would've been on this sofa sleepin' like an infant 'til sometime tomorrow."

As I dialed Auntie's number, Colby dosed off. When she answered the phone, she sounded as if she had been crying. To ease her worries, I told her that Colby was fine and at the house, asleep. She thought I was lying; thus, I shook his foot and told that nigga to say something.

"Yeah."

"I'm at his house nih. He sufferin' from migraines again."

"Is that the lie he tellin' you?"

"He's not lyin', Auntie."

"You would lie for him. Put him on the phone," she sternly commanded.

Throwing Colby the phone, he placed the phone to his ear and said, "Hello."

From his facial expression, I knew Auntie was giving him a nice set of words that wasn't allowed in the church she and Uncle Colby attended every Sunday.

Deeply inhaling, Colby softly said, "Ma, I really don't wanna do this tonight. Can you at least wait 'til my head stops hurtin'? Fuss at me then, please."

His pleas didn't work.

Clearing his throat, he calmly said, "Ma, chill, okay. I have enough on my plate as it is. These folks telling me that I have malformed veins on the right side of my brain, an' a nigga really tryin' to understand what that really mean fo' me. So, fuss at me another day, but not right now. I ain't in these streets no mo'. I'm done. I been fillin' out job apps. I got enough on my brain now without hearin' how disappointed you are in me. Ma, I love you, but I gotta close my eyes."

Several seconds later, he said, "It's called Venous angioma, Ma. I go see a neurologist tomorrow at ten o'clock at the Goode Building by Jackson Hospital."

Shortly afterwards, Colby said, "I'm going by myself."

"Okay, Ma. I'll be by the house to pick you up. Please be ready on time." He sighed before telling her goodnight and that he loved her.

Throwing the phone towards me, Colby faced the sofa and closed his eyes.

"Colby, why didn't you tell me 'bout yo' brain, man?"

"Didn't want to tell anyone 'til I knew exactly what I was up against."

"Dude, we tell each other everythin'. I would've been there to ask questions, an' be yo' rock like I've always been."

"Not this time, Grinch, not this time. It's time fo' me to let you go, so that you can be the man that you need to be fo' Zariah an' Jeremy. I got things from here. Thanks fo' savin' my ass. I owe you big time … if I don't croak ova from the V.A. shit," he said, seriously.

Not liking how he was talking, I quickly corrected his attitude.

"Don't go talkin' crazy, Colby. You gonna be just fine. You got a whole family that loves you, an' we ain't gon' let you go through anythin' by yo'self. You should know better than to think that."

"A'ight, now can you please shut the fuck up, so I can sleep?" he questioned with a smile on his face before throwing a pillow at me.

"Yeah, I can do that. I guess I'll pull out som' cover an' knock out on the other sofa."

"Do that," he stated while yawning.

After visiting the hallway closet, I came back with two pillows and a large University of Alabama cover. As I kicked off my shoes and outstretched on the sofa, Colby was snoring. Looking towards his way, I quickly thought about staying at his crib. That nigga had a way of disturbing the peace when people were trying to go to sleep.

Getting comfortable on the sofa, I researched the condition with Colby's brain. Halfway through reading about the illness, I had several questions that I needed him to ask his doctor. Now, I understood why he was confused as to what the condition really meant for him.

Lord, please let my cousin be okay. He has to be okay ... not just fo' his kids, but fo' me too.

Chapter Eight

Zariah

Friday, December 7th

This has been one hell of a week. From being harassed by my father to dealing with Nene crying about the status of Colby's brain. I was a bundle of nerves as I tried to be there for everyone, including Uncle Colby. He took it the hardest, and I didn't know why until Fernando told me that Uncle Colby had some harsh things to say about his son.

According to the neurologist, Colby's condition was stable and non-cancerous; yet, it was best that his pressure didn't rise to high nor should he involve himself in any extreme sports. On the contrary, none of those things really mattered. If he caught a common cold or some other winter illness, the symptoms may trigger the headaches to become more aggressive.

Fernando drove himself crazy with studying about Venous angioma and Cavernous angioma. He was determined to know all that he could about them, granted that he was at the doctor's appointment with Colby, Uncle Colby, and Auntie Maryann. From what he told me, the specialist couldn't give them more answers than what he read on the Internet. Every hour on the hour,

Fernando called Colby to check on him. He became so worrisome to his cousin that Colby popped up with two duffel bags and said that he was moving into the spare room since Fernando wouldn't let him rest.

"Look at the little princess working like the dog that she is," a familiar voice stated before laughing.

Sighing heavily, I stopped stocking and turned around to face three of Nathan's ghetto daughters, dressed to perfection in designer clothing with a face filled with makeup.

Rolling my eyes, I snapped, "Maybe you should try it instead of sucking dick and moving dope around like the do-girls that y'all are."

"Look bitch," Markesha stated sternly while clapping her hands.

"No bitch, you look, don't come up in my job harassing me. I don't want shit to do with you and your family. I would think that a group of bitches like yourselves would appreciate less competition from someone of my caliber. I would steal attention away from you tacky, goofy dressing bitches. I would make y'all feel like shit when I don't have to suck a dick or let a nigga play in my pussy just to get him on board with my father. I wouldn't have to do any of those demeaning things that Nathan got y'all doing. With that being said, I smell the stench of dope boys that just strolled into the area. Maybe y'all should go suck them off and pull them further into Nathan's crew."

Growling, the leader of the pack, Shardya, stepped into my face and shoved me against a rack. Not up for being bullied, I slapped the shit out of her and nastily spoke, "Get the fuck away from me. The next time y'all come an inch near me, you will die. This is my final warning."

"We don't give a fuck 'bout being in this sto', fuck boy. We can get it … like I told yo' ass … on sight my nigga, on sight!" a loud, deep voice man spoke as a group of guys argued.

"Y'all need to leave this store now before I call the police!" one of the front end managers loudly stated.

"We need to make our way out of here. Them Burgundy niggas finna shoot this bitch up," Shardya voiced while moving away.

"Y'all got that nigga Grinch on y'all side. Y'all are not finna take over!" one of the niggas yelled, causing me to place my hand over my mouth.

No, no, no, Fernando. Not again.

"I'm calling the police now!" Johanna, the back end manager, voiced as she ran towards the phone, inches away from my working area.

"An' we gon' take this bitch over, so get ready to be underneath our wing or die!" was the last verbal statement yelled before gunshots and screams sounded off.

Dropping to the ground, I made sure that my body was as low to the ground as I could possibly have it. An eerie scream escaped a woman's mouth. I heard that scream before; instantly, chills ran through my body. There was no doubt in my mind that someone had dropped dead near her.

As I lay on the ground, I felt as if I was in the middle of a war zone, again. Closing my eyes, I prayed that the nonsense would stop soon. My prayer went unanswered.

I gotta get the fuck out of here.

As my heart raced, the gunfire sounded as if it was coming closer to me. Opening my eyes, I saw two niggas running and holding guns that was as long as like my arm. Slowly crawling backwards, my foot hit the top of Shardya's head. She hollered, and I told her to shut the fuck up and come with me. I'd never had a reason to be nasty to them as they were to me; yet, we were family. I wouldn't sleep right at night if they were killed and I could've saved their miserable lives.

Halfway towards the other two bitches, I told them to stay low and follow me towards the back. Scared shitless, they nodded their head. As we crawled towards the stock room, a horrid scream sounded from the front of the building.

Products within the store were destroyed by gunfire. Screams and crying overwhelmed the store as my foot hit the black doors. Hopping to my feet, I hauled ass towards the opening of the back doors. Nathan's daughters were right behind me as they heavily breathed. Once outside of the building, a safe distance away from harm's way, I stopped running and bent over to catch my breath.

"Thank you for getting us out of there," Shardya stated sincerely as she looked at me.

"Now, can y'all please stop harassing me? That shit there is the reason why I don't want anything to do with the lifestyle that Nathan has put y'all in. I don't want to be in fear all of my life. I don't want anyone coming after me and my son because they want him dead. I don't hate y'all. I never did. I just don't want that lifestyle around my son and me. Nathan and Patricia have done things to me that no child should have to experience at an early age. I'm not built for that life. By the look on y'all's faces, y'all ain't built for that life, either."

Sighing heavily, they looked at each other before Markesha said, "We didn't have a choice in any of the things that we do. Nathan told us to bother you and other shit. We didn't want to, but what he says goes."

"You don't have to do everything that he says. You don't need him for money, either. I know y'all have talents that can make y'all money. Trust, I've heard of the things y'all make. Tap into that and separate yourselves from that criminal life. He only creates children to use them. Don't let him win," I told them as we heard police sirens.

Knowing that the inside of the store wasn't safe, I told them that we would not go back inside until the police had the building surrounded. Within three minutes, they had the place surrounded as four officers were approaching us.

"We do not snitch," Monia voiced, barely moving her mouth.

"Agreed," we replied before inhaling deeply. There was no way I was going to say a word anyways since those guys had Fernando's name in their mouths.

When the officers arrived in our faces, the questions began. We poorly answered them as we played our part of not knowing a thing. As soon as they left, we walked back inside of the building. I was over working; Fernando was the only person that I wanted to see. We had a lot to talk about. He was in some heavy shit, and I didn't want to be a part of it.

"Are you okay?" my supervisor asked in a calm tone.

"No," I replied.

"We are closing the store early. Whenever the police allow us to leave, we are all going home. The store will re-open Tuesday," she stated as I saw the coroner placing a customer inside of a body bag.

"How many people injured?" I found myself asking.

"Two."

"How many are dead?"

"Seven, including one of our workers."

"Who?"

"Trina McClain."

My knees buckled as I asked her to repeat herself again.

"Trina McClain."

"Oh God," I said as I placed my hand over my mouth and dropped to the ground.

"Are ... were you and her close?"

Nodding my head, I said, "We were heading that way. She was pregnant."

"My God," was all that she could say as I cried into my hands.

My cell phone vibrated. It was a call, and I was sure that it was Fernando. As I retrieved my phone, my supervisor said some comforting words as my sisters rubbed my back.

"Hello," I cried.

"Aye, are you okay?"

"Noo. I'm not okay."

"Are you hurt? What in the fuck went on?" he rapidly questioned.

"Not physically hurt, baby, not physically hurt. Where are you? Who are you with?"

"I'm in the parkin' lot of Best Buy, an' I'm wit' Gun'em."

"Babyyy," I cried out before delivering the bad news to him.

"What?" he asked in an alarm tone.

"Trina's dead."

Silence overcame the phone as I heard Gun'em asking employees about Trina. Several people told him that they hadn't seen her since the shooting started, but that they were sure that she was fine.

"Baby, did you hear me?" I asked.

"Yeah," he softly said before calling for Gun'em to come to him.

"I'mma go ask one of these officers 'bout my guh, bruh. I'll be right back."

"How fast can you get out of that door, Zariah? This blow finna push him over the edge. I can't do this alone, baby … I can't." Fernando sighed.

Hopping to my feet, I said, "I'm on my way out of the front door."

Keeping my head forward, I refused to look at the catastrophe around me. I didn't want to see this nightmare in my dreams tonight. Halfway towards the door, I saw my supervisor talking to a coroner while standing over a covered body.

"Her name is Trina McClain, and she was pregnant. She worked here," was all that I heard as my eyes were on Gun'em and Fernando.

Walking through the doors as if I was a zombie, my heart went out to the guy that was in love with a woman who was carrying his first child. I didn't know if I had the courage to tell him that they were about to bring the love of his life out in a body bag. I knew that he wouldn't be the same again. This careless incident was going to bring out a side of him that no one would be able to tolerate, not even Fernando.

"Hey Zariah, have you seen Trina?" Gun'em asked me anxiously as he at the destroyed electronic store.

I looked at Fernando and nodded my head. Once Fernando moved to the back of Gun'em, I looked at my sisters and mouthed for them to sneakily surround Gun'em. As soon as they did so, I hopped in front of him and placed his hands on my face.

"What y'all doing?" He laughed. It wasn't a humorous laugh.

"Do you see those three people standing together? Two males and a female? They are going to bring Trina ou—" I stated before he aggressively began moving and shouting.

"Get the fuck off me! Get the fuck off me!" he yelled, angrily.

Police officers strolled towards us as Gun'em went berserk, but we wouldn't let him go.

"She can't ... she's pregnant wit' my child. She ain't dead, Zariah. She ain't!" he yelled, trying his best to break away from us.

Crying as my heart broke, I said, "She is gone, Gun'em, and I'm so sorry. I'm sorry."

As the officers approached us, Gun'em fell to the ground and cried his soul out. That was the first time that I had ever seen him cry.

"She was going to have my baby, mane. She was finally coming around to the idea of us being a family. What asshole would shoot up a place of business? Who decided that it was okay to take her and our child away from me?"

Placing my eyes on the officers, the look they held on their faces said a thousand words. As they slowly walked to a distraught Gun'em, my sisters slowly pulled away from him as Fernando held tightly on to his best friend.

One of the officers handed Gun'em a card while saying, "There isn't enough words that I can say to comfort you. I will give you this card, and I will be looking forward to seeing you in this coping group. I lost my pregnant wife to nonsense like this six months ago. I can't make you many promises for your broken heart, but I damn sure can make you a promise that we are going to get the bastards that did this."

Gun'em was never the type of nigga that would be caught dead communicating with a cop, but today his guard was down. He cried while reading the card. Shortly afterwards, another cop told him that he was in the coping group as well. He said that he couldn't entirely relate to their situation, but he related on the matter when it came down to his girlfriend having a massive heart attack while driving home one day from work.

A nasty growl escaped his mouth as he hollered Trina's name. His eyes were on the front door of the retail store. I knew then that they were carrying her out. It took the four officers and Fernando to push Gun'em back as he aggressively fought to go towards his deceased girlfriend. It took everything in them to get him away. When they finally controlled him, they placed handcuffs on his hands and feet.

Any other time, I wouldn't have gone for that type of treatment, but today Gun'em needed it. My love's hardcore best friend needed all the help that he could get because what those Burgundy niggas didn't know was that they unleashed a fucking insane hippopotamus out into the streets.

Mayhem has landed into the streets of Montgomery. God, be with the people in the hoods.

***

"Are you sure the Burgundy niggas kicked shit off?" Fernando asked, running his hand across his head.

Nodding my head, I replied, "Yes."

"Fuck!" he yelled as he pounded on his knee.

It didn't take a rocket scientist to know that shit was about to get real.

Clearing my throat, I looked at my man and asked, "On a scale of one to ten, how bad can things get once Gun'em learns who was behind the shooting?"

"Off the Richter scale. Those niggas will not see him comin' nor will those niggas know exactly who popped off on they asses. They have so many enemies. There will be a war in these streets."

"Who are they, exactly?"

"No need to worry 'bout that. You an' our son will be safe. I promise you that," he lightly voiced while grabbing my hand and kissing the back of it.

Sighing heavily, I asked, "Who's with Gun'em?"

"Colby an' som' of the niggas that Gun'em roll wit'. Why?"

"Just wanted to make sure that he had some people around him that will keep him halfway sane."

"Baby, can't nobody but me handle Gun'em. Those niggas aren't a match fo' him. Hell, I'm not really holdin' him down because if I was in his shoes I would've already started the war."

Silence overcame us as we gazed into each other's eyes. I didn't know what to say because I knew exactly what Fernando was thinking. He was an eye for an eye type of man. If pain was brought his way, he would make sure those that whoever brought it felt every ounce of the horrendous emotion. I had no dog in this fight; thus, I sat back and kept my comments to myself.

"It's time fo' bed. I have a long day tomorrow."

"You have to work?"

"Yeah," he quickly replied, standing and not looking at me.

Instantly, I knew he was lying. He was going to be working for a paycheck all right; his ass was going to be in the streets doing something he had no business doing. Granted with the situation that Colby placed him in, Fernando and Gun'em had some shit cooking, also.

114

"You do not have to work tomorrow, so what will you be doing?"
I asked, following him towards my bathroom.

"I told you workin', Zariah." He sighed while throwing his head
backwards and glaring at the ceiling.

"You've never kept anything away from me, so why start now?" I
lightly questioned as I placed my head on his back and wrapped
my arms around his toned waist.

"Because you don't need to know everythin' that I do. It needs to
be that way."

"No, it doesn't. We are a team, and we will always be that."

Turning around to face me, Fernando looked lovingly into my
eyes, placed a kiss on my forehead, and said, "You don't need to
worry 'bout a thing. Okay?"

"That's easier said than done. Whatever happens to you will
happen to me."

"It's been a long day. Let's go take a shower an' watch T.V. before
we go to sleep."

Ring. Ring. Ring.

Pulling his phone from the holster, Fernando quickly answered
while moving away from me.

"A'ight. Where 'bout?" he asked within several seconds of the
phone being pressed to his ear. "I'm on the way now."

"Where are you going?" I asked as he placed his phone into the
black holster.

"Gotta take care of somethin' real quick."

Before he walked passed me, I grabbed his arm and asked, "Where are you going?"

"Zariah, the less you know the better. Okay? I'll be back soon as I can."

With his statement lingering in the air, Fernando walked away from me. I couldn't move as it seemed like my worst fears were coming to life. The last time Fernando pulled away from me without telling me where he was going, he was shot six times and ended up barely clinging onto life.

Feeling as if my world was closing in, I ran to the front room and retrieved my cell phone. With shaky hands, I dialed Nene's number. Looking at the time on the DVR box, I knew that there was a possibility that she was asleep. On the eighth ring, her groggy voice answered.

"I think I'm about to have a panic attack or something," I said, instead of greeting her.

"What's wrong?"

"I think Fernando and Gun'em are up to some shit that would place me in a mental ward."

"I'm up," she replied, informing me that she was all ears.

"I can't lose him, Nene. I just can't," I softly whined as tears welled in my eyes.

"Are you at his house or yours?"

"Mine."

"I'm on the way."

"No, don't come out in this air with Colbon."

"He's with his grandparents."

"Okay."

"So, once again, I'm on my way."

Nodding my head, I replied okay before ending the call.

Fifteen minutes later, Nene walked through my front door with her purple and pink bonnet on her head and Christmas-themed long-sleeved pajama set clinging to her body. With a raised eyebrow, I looked at my friend and chuckled while shaking my head.

"Look, I didn't have time to put on clothes. Therefore, don't you be laughing at me. Now, let's get down to talking," she said while walking towards the sofa I was sitting on.

After we hugged, the talking began. I expressed to my friend how I was afraid of losing the only man that I'd ever loved. Through tears and sobs, I told her my worst fears for my family and friends. Everything that I wanted to tell Fernando before he left, I dropped it into Nene's lap.

Afterwards, she stared at me and said, "You are in a tougher position than I am in. I honestly don't know what to tell you other than pray. Thanks to Colby's ass, we are in a box that could destroy everything that we have dreamt of having. If it wasn't for this pregnancy and Colbon, I wouldn't be talking to him."

"Speaking of Colby, have you talked to him?"

"Nope. He doesn't call me, and I don't call him. I learned that he bought Colbon a phone. At least he's not turning his back on our son."

"You should call him," I voiced as I heard Fernando and Gun'em frantically talking.

Hopping to our feet, Nene and I were at the door in record time. As she opened it, a sight came to our eyes that damn near crippled Nene as I ran out the door.

"Nene, call 911 … now!" I yelled as I poorly tried to assist the fellas with a convulsing Colby.

"What in the fuck happened to him?" Nene cried from inside of my home.

"Hold him tight. Make sure he doesn't bite his tongue off," I stammered, not knowing if I was right or wrong.

It seemed as if it took the ambulance forever to arrive at my home. When they did, my nerves were shaken as they checked Colby out. The EMT's asked several questions that each of us answered according to the knowledge that we knew.

As they placed Colby on a stretcher, I told Fernando and Gun'em to be there when he arrived at the hospital and that we were on our way. Quickly running to my son's room, I dressed him comfortably. Nene was on the phone with Colby's parents.

Ten minutes later, we were ready to go when a knock sounded off at my door. Without thinking to ask who it was, I opened the door and stared a straggly bitch in the face.

"And what in the fuck do you want?" I asked Maleeka.

"Your life ... the one that you have with Grinch," she stated with a sneaky smile on her face.

Angrily, I spat "Get the fuck off my property, bitch!"

"I'm sure your presence is needed at the hospital. I just wanted to stop by and tell you that I will have him sooner than later. You don't have him under your grasps as you think. He just left my home."

Nene brushed past me, knocking the broad into the plastic chairs on my porch.

"Nobody has time for your shit. If Fernando wanted you, he would've made you his baby momma. Now, get the fuck on before you be at the hospital in a special unit for people that are clinging onto their lives."

Maleeka was scared of Nene; thus, she didn't say anything or move. Nene gathered as much spit as she could before spitting in Maleeka's face.

Laughing, that heifer wiped it off and said, "You and your man have a thing for spit, huh? Oops, I forgot, Colby isn't your man anymore. I should know."

Nene was ready to pounce on Maleeka until I reminded my best friend that we had better things to do.

Giggling as she walked off my porch, Maleeka stopped and looked at me before saying, "Zariah, I picked your man up in front of your home. He knows that we don't like each other, yet, he did the one thing a man who's *supposedly* in love with his girl should never do. Don't be blind to the facts, sweetheart. He hasn't popped the question for a reason. Don't be dumb for him all of your life. Damn, didn't your mother teach you anything? Oh, yeah ... that's right ... she's dumb for Nathan. How can she teach you anything when she's sucking pussy, ass, and titties for a nigga that's in love with her supposed friend? Whew, chile, y'all Nash bitches super dumb for the dick."

Closing and locking my door, I couldn't focus on the idiot in my presence. She was more irrelevant now than she was during our school days. A bitch of her caliber would do anything to get under my skin and in bed with my man. However, two things she said were accurate.

As I walked down the steps with my son sitting comfortably in his car seat, I glared into Maleeka's face with a huge grin. While I started the engine, Nene angrily talked and strapped Jeremy in the back seat. I didn't respond to anything that she said. My mind was in another place—Fernando's car.

As I stared at his pearl white, new model Cadillac, I walked towards the hood. Placing my hand on top of it, I laughed. If he had driven it, it should've still been hot, but it wasn't.

Nawl, Fernando would not be in her presence. What reason would he have to be other than to get closer to Poboy and his crew? After all, the grimy bitch knew everything about every street nigga. There is no way that he would be fucking around with her; however, in order to keep the bitch in her place, he had to be giving her something.

Taking a seat in my car as I placed the gearshift in reverse, Nene asked, "I know damn well you aren't entertaining the shit that Maleeka said?"

With a fake smile on my face, I calmly replied, "Hell no. I know Fernando's indiscretions, and him fucking with bitches is not one of them."

Chapter Nine

Grinch

Saturday, December 8th

Ever since Zariah dropped Jeremy off with Nanna, she had been extremely quiet. She barely looked at me. When she asked to me if I was hungry, I knew that we were headed for a severe conversation that would result in me becoming overly pissed off.

"Maleeka came by here not long after y'all left for the hospital yesterday. She had a lot to say about her picking you up from my house amongst other shit. So, why would she come to my door and make that announcement, Fernando?" Zariah asked as she placed food on my plate.

Ah shit. That bitch. That dirty, dirty bitch.

"Because I did get in the car wit' her yesterday, but it wasn't on no sex tip or anythin'. It was 'bout information that she supposedly had fo' me," I told her honestly while staring into her face.

"Hmm," she quickly replied before saying, "I find it funny that you can do something so careless like that. When were you going to tell me? Fuck that ... *were* you going to tell me?"

"Yes, but it wasn't going to be today. Once I had the next set of plans in the air I was going to tell you 'bout the information that I sought from her."

With a raised eyebrow, Zariah gave me a look that put my ass in compliance. Instantly, I was making sure that she knew I wasn't playing games. As I talked, she walked off on me, shaking her head. Her choice to ignore me caused me to call her name, sternly.

"I don't want to hear that shit you are talking, Fernando. We are supposed to be a team, but you keep shit from me. You and the streets combined is my business. You got the game fucked up if you think you are going to be up in another bitch's face, and I don't know what for until after she has the audacity to knock on my fucking door!" Zariah yelled, turning around to shove me against the wall.

"You are so cute when you yell at me." I joked, pulling her into my arms.

"I'm not playing with your ugly self. You are officially on punishment for doing shit behind my back. I swear you and Nathan are really working my damn nerves. Get the fuck out of my house!" She barked before pulling away from me.

Grabbing her wrists, I angrily asked, "What has Nathan done nih?"

"Nothing," she lied, not looking at me.

"Zariah, I'm not going to ask yo' ass again. What in the fuck has Nathan done nih?" I spoke loudly, shoving her up against her bedroom's doorframe.

"If you don't get your motherfucking hands off me like that, I know something. The best thing you can do is leave before I say some shit you really don't want to hear." She growled, cocking her head to the right.

"Zariah, what … in … the … fuck … did … that motherfuckin' nigga say to you?" I spoke through clenched teeth.

"Why, so you can confront him and do something stupid?"

"Nope. So, I can see why he's so damn nasty to you. Have a man-to-man talk. That's all I want to do. I won't put my hands or have anyone else put their hands on him. Just tell me what he said," I softly replied, placing my hands on the small of her waist.

Sighing heavily, she gazed into my eyes and slowly began telling me what Nathan said to her. She told me the more he talked, the more intense things became over the phone between them. While I listened to her, I knew I was going to put my hands on him. There was no way Nathan was going to get away with talking to my woman in a hateful manner. Once she informed me of the threat that he made against me and the future possibility of us adding another baby to our family, I fucking lost it.

As I zipped through her home, Zariah was on my heels, loudly telling me not to leave. While I ignored her, I had tons of thoughts on what I was going to do to Nathan. By the time I finished whooping on his old ass, he would be begging me to slang a bullet in his fucking dome.

After I snatched my keys off the entertainment center and stuck my feet inside of my shoes, Zariah was on her knees begging me not to leave.

"I wouldn't be yo' man if I don't leave an' go handle this shit that Nathan has started," I told her before walking out.

I stepped into the day's cold air wearing a black T-shirt and black gym shorts, ready to set some shit off. One would've thought that I would be cold, but I was far from it. My body was burning up with anger. I was eager to be in Nathan Price's presence.

Once inside of my whip, I banged on the steering wheel as I cursed Nathan out for how he made my woman feel. I couldn't understand why he did the things he did to his children; he had ten—six boys and four girls. It wasn't like he gave a fuck about any of them. He turned his sons into runners; each of those dummies did time for him and made sure that they eliminated any threats to their father. His daughters slept with the highest member of an organization he was interested in doing business with. They would transport drugs for him. One of them, Markesha, was looking at prison time for two sale cases. She could have gotten out of those cases—without snitching—but Nathan was hell bent on her serving her time.

Nathan was the type of nigga that let his family's reputation and last name get to his head. All he cared about was going down in history as a legend, right along with the rest of his deceased family members. The Price Dynasty was a motherfucker; it was created by a woman named Georgina Price in the mid-1970's. She was Nathan's great-great-great grandmother. The criminally mastermind woman created savages and money hungry individuals with her ambitions of wanting her family to be on top of the food chain. Once she died, her Dynasty went through several hands of greedy bastards and bitches.

My cell phone rang a special tune, informing me that it was Zariah calling. Pressing the ignore button, I placed the gearshift in reverse and sped away. I wanted to be on the North side of town within six minutes. That was where the Prices' rested their heads, did their dirt, and anything else people could think of.

Inhaling and exhaling, I thought of the best way to have a serious discussion with a rogue motherfucker like Nathan. Several plans had to be set in stone when I approached Nathan. I was never the type of person that committed an act without thinking of the consequences if things went wrong. My life and those that I loved were on the line, so I had to execute the right plans.

Arriving in the heart of the north side, I cruised the streets until I found Nathan's custom painted, gold with snowflakes dripping throughout the fully loaded, new model Cadillac CTS Sedan. The whip was extremely nice and worth every dime Nathan paid for it. I couldn't lie as if the old school nigga didn't have good taste in vehicles and attire. He knew this; thus, he didn't mind flexing any day of the week, even in front of twelve.

The tall, dark-skinned, skinny, fuck nigga was dressed in an ivory, linen outfit and expensive dress shoes while standing beside his car and talking to one of his flunkies. A short, pretty older woman wearing a red sweater dress and brown, knee-length boots stepped onto the porch and said something. As he faced the woman, I saw that he had a Glock stuffed in the holster.

As I pulled behind his car, the woman walked inside of the single-family, gray-bricked home. While he looked my way, I made sure that my strap was off safety and tucked it in the back of my gym shorts. When I opened the door, Nathan chuckled before dismissing the flunky.

"What do I owe the pleasure to have you, *Mr. Grinch,* in my face while I'm at one of my bitch's cribs?" Nathan's deep baritone voice asked as he fired up an Arturo Fuente Opus X, an expensive cigar.

"Shid, what's up wit' you harassin' my guh the way you do, Nathan?" I inquired while glaring into his dark-brown, medium-beaded eyes.

Chuckling, he blew smoke out of his mouth and nose before saying, "Last time I checked, I don't answer to you or any other nigga in these streets. But umm … since you beatin' down *my* daughter, I guess I can tell you a lil' som' som'. You see, I need Zariah's ole sweet an' naïve ass to transport som' dope fo' me. I need her to accept her birthright. I need all ten of my churren to do their parts. Zariah is placin' extra pressure on her brothers an' sisters because she won't do her part."

Shaking my head, I looked the nigga in the eyes and spat, "Nathan, you got enough dummies on yo' team. Leave Zariah out of it. She don't want anything to do wit' you. You already on top. You don't need her fo' anything. Feel me?" I stated through clenched teeth.

Walking closer to me as he dropped his expensive cigar on the ground, Nathan glared into my eyes as if he wanted to fight.

"Lil' boy, the best thing you can do is disappear off the face of this earth. You keep on testin' me, an' I will make that happen … just like I told *my* daughter I would do. I would hate to have you scattered across the ocean like yo' parents were." He snickered.

There were no words to be spoken after the comment that he made. Quickly, I punched that nigga in his throat. Afterwards, I whipped out my gun and placed a bullet between his eyes. Turning around, I didn't give a damn if anyone saw me or was ready to place a bullet in me. He sealed his fate the moment he talked ill about my parents. There was no way in hell that I was going to let his ass live after the slick way he talked. True enough, my actions were going to have dire consequences, but that was something I was willing to deal with.

Taking a seat in my car, I slowly peeled away from the scene with an ugly expression plastered across my face. As I cruised down the residential street, people gathered at the house where Nathan's corpse lie beside his pretty, gold-snowflake painted vehicle.

My mind told me to go to Zariah's, but my arms steered my car in Gun'em's direction. When I arrived at my partner's crib, there were cars parked everywhere. There was no doubt in my mind that Gun'em was inside his smoke-filled home concocting plans to knock of the Forge and Burgundy niggas.

Shutting off the engine and stepping out with my head held high, I had a smile on my face as if I was the true Grinch. As I walked towards the front door, I smelled quality weed. Once I opened the door and stepped inside of the single-family, older home, everything came to a halt.

"What in the fuck have you done?" everyone asked as they whipped out their guns in defense mode.

"I don't take kindly to threats or disrespect towards my family, y'all know that. I am proud to state that it will be DEFCON five 'round this bitch. I just murked Nathan ... in broad daylight ... an' I cruised away from the scene with a smile on my face," I told them as I took a half-smoked blunt out of Gun'em's hand.

"Ohh, shit," they replied in a shocked tone as their phones began to ring.

"Wit' that being said, which one of you gon' try an' knock me off?" I questioned, laughing.

Everyone, minus Gun'em, in the room associated themselves with Nathan. They didn't get special privileges, but they bought work from him. If he wanted something done, he would seek one of the niggas that were in my faces. I would say that they were scared of Nathan and his family, but that would be an understatement; they were horrified of them.

"Shid, you know I ain't gon' fuck wit' you," one of them stated, triggering the others to say the same thing.

"I'm tellin' y'all right-motherfuckin'-nih, don't come fo' me in those streets, if you won't come fo' me here. Is that clear?" I asked, looking each of them in the face.

"Crystal," they replied, nodding their heads.

"We will post up an' protect yo' shit. You an' yo' family need to get out fo' a while until we ge—"

"Nawl, what we gonna do is wipe them off the map now. I don't want shit comin' back his way or ours. So, the best thing we can do is begin rollin' out nih to murk those that will retaliate against Grinch. Understood?"

"Most definitely," they replied.

"Aye, Gun'em, I'm finna use the bathroom before I leave," I told him. That statement was coded, indicating that I was going to get my artillery that I had stashed in the back room underneath the bed.

"A'ight."

As I headed towards the bathroom, I heard the stampede of niggas leaving and talking about the areas they were going to patrol. When I made it to the room, Gun'em called my name. I didn't say a word as I dropped to my knees and snatched the white, large duffel bag and black, stainless steel gun case.

"You need to get Jeremy an' Zariah out of the city fo' a couple of days. You won't be on this mission, nigga. I don't have anythin' to lose. You do. Take my whip an' leave the city. While we handle our business with the Prices', we will take care of the Forge an' Burgundy boys. I'll let you know when y'all can enter the city. Understood?" he said sternly in a tone that I had become accustomed to hearing since the death of Trina.

"I can't let you do this alone. We have never done missions alone," I replied as I stood tall, slinging the duffel bag's strap across my right shoulder.

"You made Zariah a promise. So, honor it," he voiced before walking away.

He was right, but I felt that I needed to make sure that he lived—for me. If I didn't have my ace boon coon walking with me; then, I was going to be highly fucked up for life.

"I meant what the fuck I said, Grinch!" he yelled before tossing me his keys.

"We do shit toget—"

"I said what the fuck I said, woe! Damn it, do me this solid an' I swear after this shit here ... I'll do anythin' you ask of me. Deal?"

Sighing heavily, I wanted to protest but that special ringtone sounded on my phone.

Lying, I said, "Deal."

"Now, she's callin' you. I'm sure she's heard 'bout what happened. Get her an' my lil' woe the fuck out of this city. We finna start sprayin' today. I'll reach out to Colby an' tell him that he, Nene, an' their son needs to get to his parents' house, an' to make sure that they don't come outside fo' shit 'til I say so."

Nodding my head, I looked at my homie since grade school and said, "Fuck nigga, you make sure yo' ass make it back to us alive. Understand?"

"Nigga, I know you ain't going soft on me." He chuckled.

"Fuck you, nigga." I chuckled before continuing in a serious tone. "Much love, woe, an' do what I said ... make it back to us, alive."

I can't let you do this shit on yo' own, nigga. I just can't.

"Bet."

My phone stopped ringing only to start ringing again.

"Hello."

"You stupid son-of-a-bitch! We are fuckin' done! Do you hear me, Fernando? We are fuckin' done. You do not have your son and I in your life anym—" Zariah angrily stated before I hung the phone up in her face.

With a blank facial expression, I strolled out of Gun'em's crib with only one thought on my mind, having my niggas back as he faced one hell of a war. I couldn't entirely focus on Zariah when my world could be turned upside down by me doing the city a favor. She would have to deal with the fact that I started a war in these streets. Most importantly, MaZariah Chloe Nash knew what she signed up for when she took on the role of being with a nigga like me, Grinch.

Chapter Ten

Zariah

I couldn't believe that bastard had the audacity to hang the phone up in my face. Fernando had a lot of nerve confronting Nathan and shooting him in the face for people to witness. The amount of destruction that was sure to follow was going to leave families mourning and scared to go out in the public. That was the reason I tried my best not to inform Fernando of Nathan's recent behavior towards me. I didn't want to feel as if I was responsible for a massacre taking place in the city, mostly the Black neighborhoods and shopping centers.

As I quickly packed some of our things, I prayed that Nanna had done the same. I didn't want to wait around. Nathan's crew knew where my loved ones and I rested our heads. There was nowhere in the city that we could sleep, shit, or eat peacefully after the foolishness that Fernando created.

Looking at the clock, I sighed deeply as I zipped the bag and slung it over my shoulders. It was three-thirty p.m., and I wanted to be on the highway within twenty minutes. As I ran towards the front door, it swiftly opened and in stepped Fernando carrying our son's car seat while Nanna wasn't far behind him.

"Zariah!" he yelled as I stepped into the kitchen, shocked to see him.

Shit, he don't supposed to be here until after I escaped with my grandmother and Jeremy, I thought as he glared into my face with an evil look that only niggas in the streets had the pleasure of seeing.

"Oou, it's mighty warm in here," Nanna sarcastically stated, indicating that the temperature of my home was too hot for her.

"Nanna, what are you doing here with Fernando?" I asked, placing my eyes on her.

"He demanded that I got in the car with him. He's going to take us to a safe place."

Instantly, I felt like throwing a tantrum at her comment. How in the fuck could he possibly keep us safe when he started this shit? Repeatedly blinking my eyes, I continued walking towards the door while shaking my head at the sexy fool that stood before me, eyes roaming my body.

"Speak yo' mind instead of blinkin' yo' eyes like that," he spoke in a tone that I really hated, bossy and harsh.

"Why would I speak my mind if you are going to do what the fuck you want anyways, Fernando?" I nastily questioned as he placed Jeremy's car seat on the ground.

"Little do you know, I do listen to you, expect fo' this one time. I had no choice but to murk that nigga, Zariah."

"Whatever, Fernando. I don't want to hear anything else about this foolishness that has erupted," I stated as I placed my shaky hand on the gray handle of Jeremy's car seat.

"Foolishness?" he asked with a hint of laughter.

"Yeah, foolishness," I quickly replied before continuing, "I told you not to do anything stupid ... matter of fact, you said that you wanted to have a man-to-man talk with him. I highly remember some years ago, I told you that if you were to do something catastrophic again ... I would leave you. I guess you thought I was playing, huh? You've done one of the three things that I fear. How could you do something of this nature that would put your entire family in harm's way? In addition, you said that you love us. Us running from fear or being slayed is not love, Fernando Rogers!"

After I finished yelling at him, my hand found its way to the side of his face. The sound that erupted after my hand connected to his soft skin informed me that Fernando felt the sting that I blessed his handsome face.

Growling as he looked into my eyes, Fernando clearly and sternly spoke through his pretty, white clenched teeth, "Make that yo' last time puttin' yo' hands on me, MaZariah Chloe Nash. I did that nigga in because he had a lot of bold shit to say to the woman that I vowed I would kill an' die fo'. I want to have mo' kids wit' you an' that nigga could've easily stopped that. He really sealed his fate when he down talked my dead parents. Yes, I brought a war, an' no, I will not be participatin' in it because Gun'em was hell bent on me not joinin' this shit. He reminded me of the vow that I pledged to you an' our son. Do I want to see the Prices' an' anyone else in their camp dead? Hell yes, I do. Do I want to live without you an' Jeremy? Hell fuck no. So, I will take this L in not being in the forefront wit' my niggas."

"You've really made things har—"

Before I could finish my sentence, gunshots ripped through my home. As Nanna and I screamed while dropping to the ground, Fernando was lying on top of our son's car seat. Flashbacks from the shootout at my job caused my mind to rehash the moments when I was crouched low on the ground, praying that I made it out alive. Jeremy started wailing as Nanna prayed. Meanwhile, I was on the floor shaking like a stripper with thoughts that whoever was shooting would come into my home and finish us off. Immediately, I began panicking. Upon hearing the glass shattering in my room, I knew that we were going to die.

When tires skirted, the shooting ceased. Rising my head, I looked around the front room; it was destroyed. Holes were in the walls, furniture, and rooftop. My once beautiful home was a mess.

"Y'all alright?" Fernando questioned as tears seeped down my face.

I didn't respond to him, but Nanna did. Jeremy's cries had stopped as he looked at me. This was not the life I had in mind for him; the action that took place was the very reason why I didn't want to tell Fernando that I was pregnant.

Angrily, I spoke, "You have created this shit!"

"Calm down, Zariah. You screamin' at me ain't going to fix nothin'. Grab what you can an' let's leave." He demanded while helping Nanna to her feet.

Fernando's cell phone rang, and he quickly answered it.

"Yeah," Fernando stated into his phone while walking towards the front door.

"Nanna, we gotta get out of here ... now. It's not safe to linger in this home a minute longer," I told her as I placed my shaky hand on my son's car seat handle.

Shortly afterward I spoke to Nanna, that bastard said, "They've just hit Zariah's crib an' the cars outside. Send someone over here to scoop us up, an' make sure those fuck niggas don't get a chance to open fire at none of my other folks' spots."

I couldn't stop shaking my head if I wanted to. The anger and frustration I felt was unbelievable. I wanted to rip Fernando's head off his shoulders. He placed me in a position I never wanted us to be in, ever.

Ending the call with whomever, Fernando dialed a number while talking to me.

"Gun'em's going to come over an' get y'all out of the city. I sure as hell ain't leavin' 'til I make sure that it's safe fo' y'all to return."

Nodding my head as I plopped my ass on the floor, I began placing a barrier between Fernando and me. He did two things that I told him I would not tolerate. It was as if he wanted to be single and childfree; thus, I was going to grant him his fucking wish. He was going to regret this day for the rest of his life.

Placing my eyes on Nanna, she nodded her head before mouthing that it was time that I let Fernando go. She didn't have to tell me because the moment my grandmother told me that Fernando killed Nathan in plain sight, I knew that I had to stop thinking about a happily ever after with him. All the future plans I had in mind with the only man that I had lain with, cried over, and loved with every drop of blood in my body were no longer important to me.

Chapter Eleven

Grinch

Monday, December 10th

After Gun'em came to pick us up on Saturday, we dropped Zariah, Nanna, and Jeremy off at a hotel in Birmingham. The further they were away from Montgomery, the better it would be for them. I lost contact with Zariah six hours after I placed them in the hotel. When she didn't return any of my calls or texts, I brought my ass back to Birmingham. I couldn't stay long because I had to deaden the mess I took pleasure in creating.

"Where are they?" I loudly asked myself before biting on my bottom lip while strolling towards the elevator of Holiday Inn.

Pressing the down button on the elevator's panel, I pulled out my phone and dialed Gun'em's number. On the fourth ring, he answered.

"They left the hotel. The hotel room card was on the dresser. She won't respond to a call or text. I have no fuckin' idea where they are. Have you heard anythin'?"

"No. Colby said that Nene an' Colbon ain't at his mother's home anymo'. They slipped out in the middle of the night."

"How is that possible when we got niggas patrollin' that area? We gave strict orders that their cars can't leave the house," I stated while stepping into the elevator.

"The cars are there, but Nene an' Colbon ain't. Do you think they are wit' Zariah?"

"It's highly possible that they are, if she rented a car. Aye, I'm finna call Colby. I'll hit you back in a few."

"A'ight."

I wasn't going to call my cousin until I was inside of my whip. Instead, I called Nanna's phone. When she answered, my heart was relieved.

"Hey Nanna, are y'all safe?"

"Yes," she replied as a door closed behind her.

"Where are y'all?"

"I'm at home. Zariah, Nene, Jeremy, and Colbon are not," she said as I walked through the lobby doors of the hotel.

With a raised eyebrow, I asked, "Where are they?"

Sighing deeply, Nanna lightly voiced, "Fernando, I'm not going to tell you where she is. You placed us in danger. That was not a smart thing to do with a child, Son. You knew better than that. Honey, I really think it's time for you to let my granddaughter go before you get her killed. I completely understand why you did what you did, but there was a better way of handling the situation."

I didn't want to hear any of the shit that she was spitting. I wanted to know where the fuck my girl and son were, and she was going to fucking tell me.

Growling as I made a fist, I sternly said, "Nanna, I don't want to be an asshole, but I need to know where is my guh an' son. Therefore, can you please not give me a lecture 'bout somethin' that needed to be taken care of?"

"That attitude right there is the reason why you just lost your family, Fernando. I lost my daughter to a nothing ass man that wanted the streets and everything else that comes along with it. You will stay the fuck away from Zariah and Jeremy, or you and I will have some problems. Understood?" she nastily spat.

Since I didn't want to disrespect Nanna, I ended the call without saying a single word. Hopping into my truck, I called Colby. The moment he picked up his phone, Auntie Maryann and Uncle Colby were fussing. I didn't give him time to tell me anything before I started speaking.

"Aye, Colbon an' Nene are wit' Zariah. I have no idea where they are. Nanna wouldn't tell me."

"Is that Fernando?" Uncle Colby asked angrily.

"Yes, sir," Colby replied.

"Hand me that damn phone, now!"

Uncle Colby rarely spoke sternly or punished us. He was a force to reckon with, and there would be nothing that Colby or I could say other than acknowledge that he was correct and accept our punishment.

"We can't leave our home. Thuggish niggas coming by my house every two hours checking on us. The police have been here, questioning us about your whereabouts and if you have any enemies. What in the hell is going on, Fernando?"

"Uncle Colby, I can't explain over the phone. All I can say is that I took extreme measures to ensure y'all are safe from the madness," I told him as I pulled away from the hotel's parking lot.

"You better be getting ready to pull your ass into my yard within one-damn-minute!" he angrily shouted before handing Colby the phone.

"Aye, Cuz, I'm in Birmingham … you gon—"

Laughing, he said, "Let me guess, I gotta take the heat 'til you get here?"

"Yep," I replied with a smile on my face.

"Well, let me go get the belt then. I swear we finna get a whoopin' up in this piece." He joked.

In the background, Uncle Colby yelled, "I'm close to putting my foot in y'all asses! All this fucking nonsense going on and not na'an one of y'all asses will tell me shit!"

"I'll put the emergency lights on an' be there within an hour … give or take."

"Aye, how are we going to find our women?"

Before I could reply to his question, Uncle Colby spat, "At least they have common sense to stop fucking with y'all knuckleheaded asses. Colby ... ugh ... get out of my face, Son."

"I'mma call you when I touch down."

"Bet."

Placing my phone in my lap, I sighed heavily as I pondered where my girl and son were. Zariah was a strong woman, but I still had to look out for her. For me to know that she wasn't in the hotel that I put her in made my head hurt. I didn't want to think negatively; thus, I focused on the positive—they were out of harm's way.

Ever since the shooting, I thought it was best to use the rest of my vacation days. My supervisor was still under the impression that there was sickness within my immediate family, and I didn't let him think anything less. I was not going back to work until I made things right with my girl. She thought she was going to leave me; she was dead wrong. I know that I told her that I was done with the street life and I meant it, but shit went left the moment Colby pulled his stunt.

One thing about Zariah was that she knew that I had mad love for her and that I would do anything to keep in her my life. In the same token, she knew what type of nigga I was when it came down to my loved ones. I would go above and beyond to ensure they were safe. I couldn't save my parents, but I felt that it was my duty to look after my loved ones.

An hour and five minutes of thinking about the love I had for my people, my mind went silent as I had to be alert. Heading towards my aunt and uncle's house, I received a phone call from Gun'em that damn neared made me hit a vehicle in front of me.

"She did what?" I asked loudly as I hopped off the nearest exit, aiming for his crib.

"Mane, that bitch wiggin'. On life, I'm thinkin' 'bout shootin' her ass in the face."

"Don't do shit 'til I get there," I voiced sternly as I banged on the steering wheel.

"A'ight. How far out are you?"

"I'll be pullin' up in ten minutes."

"A'ight," he said before we ended the call.

Performing breathing exercises like Zariah taught me, I called Colby. He had to know that something important came up to the point I wasn't able to chat with Auntie Maryann and Uncle Colby. On the third ring, he answered.

"Mane, where the fuck you at?" he whispered as I overheard Uncle Colby going off.

"I gotta stop by Gun'em's crib. Mane, Patricia doing the fuckin' most."

"Ah, shit. Go handle that."

"Bet," I stated before ending the call as I zipped off Perry Hill Road exit.

The shit Gun'em told me had my forefinger itching to press the trigger of my prized weapon. Patricia's raggedy ass visited a detective at the precinct and snitched. She took pride in telling folks around the community that I was going to prison for the murder of Nathan. I couldn't understand a woman of her caliber. The same energy that it took to snitch on me was the same energy she should've put into being a mother to her child.

After passing five red lights, I made a left turn into Forest Hill community. Zooming down the road, I made a rapid stop as I poorly parked on the curb in front of Gun'em's home. Quickly shutting off the engine and stepping out of my whip, I ran to my partner's door. The door was slightly open as cigarette smoke escaped the home. Not bothering to knock, I announced who was and stepped inside the smoky room.

As I closed and locked the door behind me, I spoke to Gun'em and two of his cousins, Damon and Monk. While they greeted me, I glared at Zariah's mother, whom was tied to a wooden chair with a white sock stuffed in her mouth. Her weave was tangled, and her makeup was awful. Shaking my head at the trash, I chuckled and strolled towards her.

"So, you wanna be a snitch, huh?" I nastily questioned as I slapped Patricia across her face. I made sure that my palm connected with her damn nose.

"Oou, shit!" the fellas yelled before laughing.

"Aye, Gun'em, it's the holiday season, ain't it?" I asked with a wicked smile on my face.

"Hell yes. You feelin' givin', my nigga?" he questioned as he walked towards his black radio.

"An' you motherfuckin' know it."

"I think I know just the song that will put you in the mood, woe."

"Play that shit … play that shit," we chanted while jigging.

The beat of "What Do The Lonely Do At Christmas" by The Emotions dropped, and I put on a performance like no other. Busting out in Zariah's favorite dance, I did that. Singing evilly to Patricia, I did that. Swirling around to the fellas, I did that. They joined in on my foolishness and like the niggas that we were; our silliness took over before I brought the stinging finale to Patricia.

At the closing of the song, I savagely pulled Patricia's head back and sinisterly sang, "Ah, what do they do … what do they do."

The song went off and I said, "A lot of shots."

Shortly afterwards, Gun'em played 21 Savage's "Close My Eyes". From there, I freely allowed Grinch to surface. I was raised to respect and honor women. It was true that Patricia possessed womanly features, but I didn't view her as a female that I should respect or honor. I'd never had the pleasure of seeing her make Zariah, Nanna, or Jeremy smile. I never had a good vibe whenever the bitch was in my presence; thus, I did the bitch bad as if she owed me some money.

I was taught never to put my hands on a woman; however, the bitch that was laying on the floor bleeding had done the ultimate no-no. I didn't give a fuck if I did kill the nigga that used her trashy ass. In my eyes, she deserved to be buried beside the nigga. I whooped on Patricia for old and new, concerning my girl. The shit Patricia put Zariah through at an early age came to my mind and I took off my belt.

I motioned for Gun'em to turn the radio down. When he did, I made an announcement to Patricia. "I'm finna whoop yo' ass like Nanna should've did. You gon' feel this *real* leather belt, bitch. You gon' apologize to Zariah fo' the shit you did to her, an' you gon' apologize to yo' mother. You most definitely gon' take yo' funky, cold pussy ass down to the police station an' take that fuckin' statement back. If you don't bitch, I'mma kill you my-motherfuckin'-self. You know I don't have any problems murkin' motherfuckas. Damn, this the most words I have ever given a pussy motherfucka before I whooped them wit' my belt."

After I looked at Gun'em and motioned for him to turn the radio up, I snatched the sock out of Patricia's mouth. My facial expression was that of The Grinch as I slammed the belt across her face before raining it down on every part of her body. I took pleasure in seeing tears stream down her face as she wiggled on the floor. My soul was happy as her screams went unheard. I continued the punishment until she passed out.

148

Placing my eyes on Gun'em, I signaled for him to cut the radio off.

Once he did, I sighed heavily and rubbed my hand across my head followed by asking, "Which one of y'all got that boy?"

"Oou shit ... things finna get spicy in the city wit' a whole whorish-junky on the loose." Gun'em chuckled as he fired up a blunt.

"Shid, I do," Damon and Monk stated in unison.

"Good. Damon, hand me a nice amount to shove into this bitch's arm. Monk, you'll give her another fix 'round the next fienin' time. What's the ticket fo' y'all product?"

"It's on the house," they replied.

"Nawl, I don't do that on the house shit ... so, what's the price?" I questioned seriously as I pulled out a wad of cash.

After they gave me their price for the purchase of heroin, I received the product and a needle. Within three minutes, I shot the potent dope into her arm. Seeing that my job was done, I looked at Gun'em and told him to make sure that she didn't leave until the bruises and welts were gone from her body, and to make sure that she did everything that I demanded.

"Bet. Be safe an' call me the second you make it to yo' destination."

"That's a bet," I voiced as I dapped him up followed by dapping up Monk and Damon.

On my way towards my whip, Colby rang my line. Immediately, I answered.

"Aye, woe, they are shootin' over this way ... don't come," he stated in a tone that informed me that he was bent low.

"Fuck!" I yelled.

Dipping back into the house, I told the fellas that it was time for us to ride out. I couldn't take another night without murdering every person that was in my way of me being a legit person for my family. Once we had Patricia's drugged up, unconscious ass secured in the back bedroom, we dipped towards my folks' side of town.

"I'm not waitin' another minute to have all these niggas dead, ya' understand?"

"Most definitely," they replied as I skirted away from Gun'em's home.

Along the way, I prayed to the Man above that the war would end quickly. It seemed with every second that passed, I was getting lost in the streets. I didn't want to get caught up in the foolishness any longer. I wasn't up for being in charge of connecting my old plugs and my partners together. That would mean I would be responsible for my homies if they fucked up.

Ring. Ring. Ring.

My thoughts ceased the moment Gun'em's phone rang. With my eyes on the road, I made sure to eavesdrop on the call.

"Who got hit?" my partner asked as I mashed on the gas pedal.

"A'ight," he replied before ending the call.

Looking at me, Gun'em said, "Yo' folks hood is hot as fuck. One of the runners said to not enter. It's not wise to go since we have artillery that the military use. So, what you wanna do, Grinch?"

"What 'til it dies down ... then we will go." I sighed as the driver's and passenger side mirrors flew onto the interstate.

There were no words spoken as Damon, Monk, and Gun'em began shooting back at a new model, white Tahoe truck with tinted windows. As my heart raced, I made sure to swerve from lane to lane to make sure whoever was in the truck didn't get the best of us. I wasn't going to die, and neither were them.

Speeding, I had to find the perfect area to box them niggas in. As I approached a split on the interstate, I choice to get off on Day Street Exit. I was guaranteed to find a street that would be suitable for my plans. With a wicked smile on my face, I dipped into a neighborhood that would be perfect for me to execute the plans.

"We finna murk them niggas!" I yelled, even though my crew couldn't hear me.

Shots after shots left my whip before I realized a group of kids was outside playing in the road. Instantly, I didn't know what to do other than to make sure those niggas wouldn't leave my son fatherless. Thus, I did what I had to do.

The Grinch That Stole My Heart

Chapter Twelve

Zariah

Two days without a man that had been in my life since
kindergarten had me wanting to pull out my hair and scream. The
more I thought about Fernando, the more I wanted to be
underneath him. I longed to be in his muscular arms as he planted
kisses on my forehead all the while professing his love for our son
and me. The warmth of his breath against my neck would make my
entire body tingle as I happily displayed my teeth. I needed to be
near him to feel alive; yet, I had to pull away.

Fernando was involved in dangerous activities that could cost us
our only son's life. The thought of anything happening to our
sweet, chunky boy caused my heart to skip beats as I felt the worst
pain a mother could ever feel. With those thoughts alone, I knew
that I wouldn't be able to forgive Fernando or myself if anything
happened to Jeremy.

"Whew, chile. I'm so hungry," Nene stated while looking at me.

Chuckling, I jokingly replied, "I'm so ready for you to have that
baby ... you eat every-damn-twenty minutes. What are you
feeding? A dinosaur?"

"I believe so." She laughed.

"You can drive the car to get something to eat. I don't want to bother Jeremy. He's sleeping comfortably."

"Alrighty," she replied looking at me.

Instantly, I saw sadness in her beautiful, medium-beaded, and dark-brown eyes. Her mind was boggled just like mine. We were on edge with all the madness going on. Neither of us wanted to visit our loved ones in jail or bury them. Minimal conversation took place since we arrived in Birmingham. We couldn't focus on T.V. or enjoy social media like we did prior to Fernando killing Nathan.

Colbon's phone rang for the twentieth time in ten minutes. It was Colby; he had been calling ever since earlier this morning, two hours after I picked Colbon and Nene up from Colby's parents home.

"Is that your dad?" Nene asked her son, whom looked just like Colby.

Nodding his head, he replied, "Yes ma'am."

"Do you want to talk to him?"

"Yes, ma'am," he replied, looking sad.

"You can answer, but don't tell him where we are ... okay?"

"Why can't Daddy know where we are, Mommy?"

"Because he doesn't need to know," she softly told her son while rubbing his head.

Exhaling deeply, Colbon answered the phone. If I knew Colby like I thought I did, he was going to ask his son as many questions as he could. Turning down the T.V., Nene and I remained silent as Colbon talked to his father. The less noise Colby heard in the background, the better.

"I'm not supposed to tell you where we are, Dad."

Shortly afterwards, Colbon replied, "Okay."

As Colbon handed his mother the phone, she shook her head and mouthed for Colbon to talk to him.

Putting the phone to his ear, Colbon shot off. "She doesn't want to talk."

For the next twenty minutes, they talked about guy stuff. Colbon looked carefree and happy as he chatted with his father. The smile on his face could light up a room. His once sad, gloomy eyes were bright and loving.

Instantly, sadness came over me as I thought of taking Jeremy away from Fernando. Even though my son was six-months old, I believed that he would miss the man that acted like a big baby when playing with him. I knew that I couldn't put the same happiness in Jeremy's eyes that Fernando did. I guess it was the bond that he created with our son—a different bond than what Jeremy and I had.

"I love you too, Dad. Get some rest, and I'll call you before I go to sleep," Colbon sadly voiced before ending the call.

As soon as Colbon placed his phone on the bed, he rested his head on his mother's back and said, "Mom, when are we going home? I miss my daddy."

Hearing Colbon's statement hurt me because I knew without a doubt that he missed that goofy, light-skinned, six-foot, athletic built man. Just like Fernando never missed a day out of Jeremy's life, Colby didn't miss a day out of Colbon's, including the pregnancy.

"I'm not sure yet, baby," Nene told her son as she gently rocked from side-to-side.

"Okay," he replied.

"Nene, when you get back we need to talk. Okay?"

Sharply inhaling and nodding her head, my best friend said, "Okay."

As she put on her shoes and jacket, we decided on what to eat. In a matter of seconds, Captain D's was the place we were going to pig out on. Giving her a twenty-dollar bill, my cell phone rang.

"Um, it's not your turn to pay for food," she stated as I saw Nanna's name displaying on my dirty screen.

Nodding my head, I placed the twenty into my wallet and answered my grandmother's phone call.

"Hello," I spoke as my heartbeat raced rapidly from fear of her delivering me bad news.

"Hey, baby. I'm just calling to check on y'all."

"We are okay. Nene is heading out to get us some food. Jeremy is sleep, and Colbon is watching T.V."

"Fernando called asking about you."

I knew it wouldn't be long before he contacted Nanna inquiring about me. Whenever we had a small issue, he would call my grandmother and pour his soul out. She would fall for his words every time; thus, she would call me and tell me that he should be on punishment for one day. However, this time Nanna wasn't on his side.

"What did you tell him?"

"Surely not that y'all are in the same hotel he placed us in. I simply told him to leave you alone."

When we changed rooms, I made sure to inform the receptionist not to give any information concerning my name to anyone, no matter what they had to say. Fernando had a way of getting answers by throwing money around.

"How did he take it?" I asked, placing my back against the headboard.

"Not like the Fernando that I know."

The Grinch is out, I thought as I asked, "What do you mean?"

"He hung the phone up in my face. He didn't talk softly or genuinely. It was as if he was possessed by a nasty, rude being."

He is.

"He didn't say anything disrespectful to you, did he?"

"No."

"Good. I would hate to cuss him out in the worst way."

Sighing heavily, Nanna asked, "Are you sure that you are ready to be a single mother? Are you sure that you can stand on your own two feet without Fernando?"

Shaking my head, I honestly replied, "No, but what choice do I have, Nanna? Because of his actions, my home was shot up with us in it. I warned him about the consequences if he involved us in something of that nature. He knew I was going to walk away. So, I have no choice but to be ready."

Ten minutes on the phone with Nanna had me thinking about the real reason why Fernando was back to some of his old ways. Gently placing my head on the headboard, I had some serious thinking to do.

If I wanted to follow through with my plans of leaving Fernando, I had to sever communication and avoid the sight of him. It would be hard to set my plans in motion if Fernando was constantly in my face or calling my phone. The sight of him interacting with our son would reel me in with a warm heart and a naïve mindset. I couldn't let that happen—I just couldn't.

As I thought about him, he called my phone. Without any hesitations, I sent him to voicemail. He called six times, and each time I sent him to voicemail.

"Oou, these people drive bad up here," Nene stated as she stepped across the threshold of the door with four bags from Captain D's.

"Tell me about it. That's why I didn't want to go out in that shit," I voiced as I hopped off the bed.

While we talked about nonsense, our phones rang. The look Nene and I gave each other told us who was calling our phones.

As we placed food on paper plates, I whispered to Nene, "Colbon is miserable. I really think you should head back to Montgomery or at least tell Colby where y'all at without giving him the actual location."

"I was thinking the same thing, but I don't want us in harm's way, nor do I want to leave you up here by yourself," she stated while silencing her phone as mine continued ringing.

"I'll be fine. The most important thing right now is Colbon being around his father. You and I know that Fernando, Gun'em, and Colby will keep y'all safe. Meanwhile, I need the time away and lack of communication with Fernando. I need my head clear, so that I can map out our future."

Ding. Ding.

Nene's phone chimed as mine stopped ringing. She looked at the screen and read a message. With shaky hands, she tapped twice on her phone before placing it to her ear. Something was wrong, and I had to know what it was. Slowly, I inhaled and exhaled several times while looking at the ceiling and silently asked God not to let any negative words come out of her mouth.

"What's wrong?" I questioned as my breathing became unsteady.

"There was a shooting in Colby's parents' neighborhood."

As I shook my head, I placed my hand over my mouth and said, "Please don't tell me anyone was hurt."

Hey. What's going on?" she asked into the phone while shaking her head at me.

The relief that flooded through my body caused me to sigh. I couldn't take knowing that someone I knew well was harmed because of who my father was.

"How long is this mess going to last, Colby?" Nene questioned lowly.

I hope not long, I thought as Nene said, "I don't want to tell you where we are. I don't want that fuckery around us. I'll answer the phone from here on out, but I will not tell you where we are, nor will I be coming back down there until the shit is over with."

Ring. Ring. Ring.

As my eyes landed on my phone, I pondered if it was Maryann or Fernando calling. Regardless who it was, I wasn't answering. I didn't want to talk to anyone but my grandmother and Nene. They were the only ones that understood my wants. Moreover, they wouldn't be down my neck telling me that I need to be doing everything in my power to cease Fernando from engaging in activities that would either place him in jail or six-feet-deep.

I adored Maryann, but she placed so much pressure on me that it was unbelievable. There had been plenty of times I wanted to tell her that I wasn't Fernando's mother nor was I his guardian growing up, but I wouldn't dare hurt her feelings because she genuinely loved Fernando and always welcomed me into her home.

Hearing Nene compassionately and lovingly talking to Colby like I did Fernando caused me to press the voicemail icon. Sighing heavily with my phone pressed to my ear, I gazed at my sleeping son. The moment the first of Fernando's message played, he was extremely upset as he asked where I was. Message after message, Fernando's tone and words changed. He went from being a bossy, semi-cold individual to a caring, submissive person. My loving man had tears streaming down my face as he professed his undying love for our son and me.

At the end of his thirtieth message, my shaky finger dialed his number. On the second ring, he answered.

"A nigga gots mad love fo' you, MaZariah Chloe Nash," he softly stated in a defeated tone.

Gently rubbing our son's head as tears flowed down my face, I softly replied, "A guh gots mad love fo' you, Fernando Gerald Rogers."

Chapter Thirteen

Grinch

Saturday, December 15th

"I called you here because I wanted you to understand that I'm not mad at you for getting Colby out of that jam. Fernando, I know that you care for my granddaughter and great-grandson, but I love them more than anything in this world. Zariah told me that your back was against the wall. However, how many times will you keep bailing out Colby and placing my precious family members in harm's way?" Nanna asked as she took a seat next to me.

"Nanna, I don't just *care* about Zariah an' our son. I love them. You know I will move mountains an' oceans fo' them. I would never want anythin' bad to happen to them. Y'all won't have to worry 'bout anyone comin' after y'all anymo'. All that beefin' is just 'bout ova wit'," I told her as she sipped from a large, snowman coffee cup.

"For how long? Until Colby finds himself doing something else stupid? Or until Gun'em needs you concerning his feelings over the loss of his girlfriend?"

Not feeling the lecture she was trying to give me, I placed my hand on Nanna's and said, "I don't mean no disrespect, but my dealin's wit' niggas that could do or bring harm to my loved ones is no concern of yours. Just know that, I'll do anythin' to keep them an' you safe. Haven't I always?"

With her lips tightly balled, Nanna nodded her head.

"I talked to Zariah som' nights ago. She told me that she didn't want to be wit' me anymo', an' it hurt like hell, but I knew the consequences the moment Poboy gave me an ultimatum. I knew that if I chose to save my auntie, uncle, an' Colby that I would risk losin' Zariah an' our son. I'm not going to stop fightin' fo' them Nanna, an' honestly I don't care how many times you summon me ova here to persuade me to leave them alone. I will not because I love them just that much. I don't see myself not wakin' up happily knowin' that I got a child that depends on me, as well as Zariah. When I say I'm done wit' the streets, I mean that. I'm sure you watched the news. You know what's going on. You know who's dead an' who's responsible fo' it."

Clearing her throat as she looked into my eyes, Nanna said, "If anything happens to them, just know that it will be on your hands, Fernando."

Feeling myself turning into a being that I didn't need to be in front of Nanna, I nodded my head and stood.

With a pleasant look on my face, I said, "They will be fine. Is there anythin' that you need while I'm on this side of town?"

"No," she replied with an attitude as she looked at the T.V., which was playing *Murder She Wrote.*

"Okay. Don't hesitate to call me if you need anythin'," I told her as I walked towards the door.

"Mm hm."

From the moment, I stepped into her home, the vibe between us was off, and I surely left her home with the same hostile vibe in the air. I wasn't going to beg her to understand why I did what I did. As long as she knew that I cared deeply for my family, I was good with that. Like I told Zariah, I wasn't going anywhere. If she left the state, I was going to find her.

Nanna and Zariah had me fucked up if they thought I was going to tuck my tail and go on about my business as if I didn't want my family. If those were their thoughts, then they really didn't know who the fuck I was. I wasn't about to let another nigga have my family when I was the best man for them.

I never left them alone to fend for themselves. I was the nigga that purchased menstruation shit for Zariah when she first stepped into womanhood. I was with her when it was time for her to have her annual checkups. Whatever she went through something, so did I. I wasn't anything like the niggas that I hung out with. Zariah had me wrapped around her fucking fingers.

Plopping into my front seat, I sighed heavily as I dialed my baby's number. On the fourth ring, she sent me to the voicemail; thus, I called her again. Her beautiful voice and Jeremy's cries graced the phone.

"What's wrong wit' Daddy's baby?" I inquired with a smile on my face as I started the engine on my truck.

"Mad because Nene won't give him any applesauce," she spoke blankly.

"He loves that shit even though it do him bad," I said before continuing, "Why are you talkin' in that manner?"

"I'm stressed, Fernando."

"Talk to me, baby," I replied as I reversed out of Nanna's driveway.

"There's nothing left to say. I said all that I needed to say to you," she spoke in a hostile tone.

"Do you really want me out of yo' life?" I asked in an agitated timbre.

She didn't respond right away; thus, I asked the question again.

"Yes and no, Fernando."

"You ain't finna put me on an emotional rollercoaster because you keep thinkin' 'bout what could go wrong in the future ... which is absolutely shit but positive things. I can promise you that."

"You and I both know that you can't make a promise of that nature," she nastily spat before continuing, "Look, what did you call me for exactly?"

"Mane, who in the fuck do you think you talkin' to like that, Zariah? Now, I know the situation that occurred got yo' mind all over the place, but don't get it twisted like you can talk to me out the side of yo' neck. I ain't wit' that shit … at all. We ain't been doing that shit an' we sure as fuck ain't finna start it. I respect you, you respect me. I'on get nasty wit' you, an' you damn sure ain't finna get nasty wit' me. Understood?" I growled, exiting out of Nanna's yard.

"Yeah," she replied, smacking her mouth.

"Now, can we talk like civilized people?"

"Yeah."

Instead of us talking about our relationship, she inquired about her nothing ass mother and what the streets had to say about her.

"Well, Zariah, you knew it was bound to happen. Yo' momma wanna be in the hottest dope boy's face. Shid, half of them niggas on that dope just to stay up to make mo' money. What did you expect from her?"

"Not to be a junkie … that's for damn sure."

"How do you feel 'bout her being on that dope?"

Sighing heavily, she softly replied, "I feel sorry for her. After all, she is my mother and I've always wanted nothing but the best for her. There would be no me without her or Nathan."

Even though I cared less to hear anything about her parents, I still asked my woman questions about her feelings for them because they somewhat mattered to her.

"How do you feel 'bout what happened to Nathan?"

Chuckling, she replied, "I think you know the answer to that one."

"In that case, yes I do. Have you talked to yo' momma?"

"Yeah. She called asking for money of course."

With a raised eyebrow, I said, "I know damn well you ain't send her no money."

"Hell fuck no. Patricia can't get shit out of me. Period! She fucked that up when she almost placed me in the foster care system in Georgia."

Tired of talking about her parents, I had the perfect opportunity to change the subject when she went quiet.

"So, tell Mr. Grinch what you want fo' Christmas?" I sexily asked.

"See, you on some more shit right now, and I'm not with it." She giggled.

It was the type of giggle that informed me that her mind was relaxed and that she was back to being my Zariah.

"You know you wit' it, so play along wit' me," I moaned as my man woke up.

"No, Fernando, I will not," she shrieked before laughing.

"Tell Mr. Grinch what you want fo' Christmas, Mrs. Grinch?" I asked as a wonderful thought crossed my mind.

"Mm, let me see," she stated before taking a pause. "I want Mr. Grinch to understand that I'm not a toy to be played with, and that I will love him until there isn't an ounce of breath in my body. I want Mr. Grinch to understand that if I chose to end our relationship ... I will not keep our son away from him."

With an ugly facial expression, I was silent. The game didn't go the way I had hoped.

"Zariah, that's not what I wanted to hear from you."

"Well, what you want me to say?"

"What you want fo' Christmas, woman. That's what," I stated as my erection was no longer present.

"If you are seeking for me to be nasty at a time like this, then you really don—"

"Imagine this ... Jeremy is asleep in his room. I got sex jams playin' at a nice decibel, yo' favorite scented candles are lit, *real* rose petals on the floor an' the bed. You are lyin' butt asshole naked underneath a Christmas tree in my room, right beside a gold tray that has different types of preserves and syrups. I place those items on yo' sexy, chocolate body an' take my time lickin' them off all the while watching you. Imagine me spreadin' yo' legs an' tastin' the sweetest dessert a nigga ever had the pleasure of devourin'. Imagine me holdin' you as yo' back arched into the perfect position while you cum in my mouth."

"My God," she softly cooed.

"Imagine me slidin' one finger than two inside of yo' cave as I passionately yet eagerly bring you to one of many orgasms. Yo' coos, groans, an' whimpers will float 'round the room as if it was the smoke from one of my blunts—lingerin' an' gettin' me high. I let you bust in my mouth several times before draggin' my long, pink tongue towards yo' mouth. The same mouth that I will take pleasure in shovin' my tongue into. As I do so—"

"Milawd, Fernando, shit just got real," she stated breathlessly as I heard a fan whirring in the background.

Laughing, I continued talking dirty to my woman.

When I pulled into my driveway, I requested for Zariah to video chat with me. When she accepted, she was blessed with the sight of my dick.

"Fernando!" she yelled as her eyes grew big.

"What?" I laughed.

With a raised eyebrow as she licked her lips, she commanded, "Stroke him for me, Mr. Grinch."

"Nawl, you stroke him."

"I'll think about it."

"There's nothin' to think 'bout, Zariah. Tell Daddy where you at so that he can hold an' kiss on you before puttin' you to sleep," I growled, putting my dick into my pants.

"Pull him back out, Fernando!" she loudly spat.

"I'll pull him out when you let yo' mind go from wantin' to leave me," I voiced while shutting off the engine and stepping out of my whip.

The wind blew so hard that I ran inside of my crib. Jack Frost wasn't playing with anyone today; thus, I didn't have any plans of coming outside anymore today unless Zariah was going to tell me where she was.

"You know how to kill a vibe, huh?" she spat in a disappointed tone.

Opening my door, I asked, "You think you just gon' up an' leave me? If you think that, then you are not thinkin' wisely, my dear."

As I stepped into my home, a horn sounded three times. Looking at my driveway, I saw Gun'em's whip parking beside my truck.

"Aye, baby, I'mma call you back. Gun'em in the yard," I told her as I closed my door.

"Don't get into no shit, Fernando," she announced with attitude.

"I won't. I love you, MaZariah Chloe Nash," I sincerely told her as I descended the steps.

"I love you, Fernando Gerald Rogers."

After ending the call, I shoved my phone into my jacket and opened Gun'em's passenger door.

"What up?" I asked as we dapped each other up.

"Shit. Cruisin' the streets to check on the progress of things from last night," he voiced before yawning.

"Details, please."

"The streets somewhat calm. With the Forge an' som' of the Burgundy niggas knocked off, there is less stress in these streets. Of course, the Prices' are still an issue fo' you. I got word that they tryin' to come fo' you hard, but not 'til the rest of the Burgundy camp is underneath their wing."

"How many went under their wing so far?" I inquired as I retrieved a cigarette and lighter from my pants, back pocket.

"Seven."

"Well, I guess we need to come up wit' a plan fast before the others join them."

"What do you have in mind fo' these niggas?"

"Not sure right now. Let's go inside an' draft up somethin' real good. Hit up Colby an' tell him to come through," I told him as he shut off the engine.

"I already chopped it up wit' him. He ain't gon' move nothin' at the moment. That nigga got a headache. Ole pussy nigga," he stated in a jokingly manner.

"That migraine he havin' is a motherfucka, mane. I don't know what I was thinkin' 'bout tryin' to have him come ova here," I said, opening the door and stepping into the cold air.

Laughing, Gun'em said, "All he need is som' high priced over-the-counter migraine pills, an' then he can kiss that shit goodbye."

"It ain't that simple, woe. Colby seein' a neurologist 'bout that migraine. Cuz got malformed veins on the right side of his brain that maybe causin' those headaches. He stressed the fuck out 'bout that. From now on out, we don't call him fo' anythin' other than to check on him."

"Damn, I ain't know he had all that goin' on. What the specialist sayin'?" he questioned as we stepped into my warm home.

"Righteously, not shit other than the risks an' talkin' 'bout other appointments to see the actual nature of his issue."

"So, it's not cancerous?"

"Nawl."

"That's good then."

With the Prices' still at me, I didn't have time to discuss Colby's health condition. I would have ample time to fill Gun'em in once shit ended with my enemies.

Sighing heavily, I said, "Now, it's time to discuss getting' those fuck niggas gone fo' life. Which one of them niggas are we going to start wit' first?"

Chapter Fourteen

Zariah

The second after I placed my phone on the bed, it rang. Looking at the unknown number, I was skeptical of answering the phone; however, something in my soul told me to answer the phone. Sighing heavily, I answered the call.

"Zariah," Shardya whispered.

With a frown on my face, I asked, "Yeah. Why are you whispering?"

"Because I don't want Dougie to hear me."

Dougie was our oldest brother; the one that didn't mind terrorizing me whenever he had the pleasure of placing his eyes on me.

"What's wrong?" I asked in a worried tone.

"He's out to kill Grinch. He's setting things in motion wit' the remaining niggas of the Burgundy crew," she quickly spoke in a whispered tone.

"What!" I stated more so than asked.

"You need to reach out to Grinch and let him know that tonight, well in a few minutes, they will be setting him up. They are going to kill him, Zariah."

"Why are you helping me?" I asked quizzically.

"Because it's time that I do. Now that Nathan is dead, Markesha, Monia, and me can be free of this shit. We can lead the lives we always dreamed of."

"If you are on some shit, Shardya, I swear I will murk you myself. Under—"

"Shut the hell up, Zariah, and do what I told you to, that's if you want to save him. If not, then keep going back and forth with me."

"Okay ... okay," I spoke in a panicked tone as I ran my hand through my burgundy, silky hair.

"Hurry, his time is running short," she spoke before ending the call.

Clearing my throat as my shaky finger dialed Fernando's number, I demanded Nene to pack their things.

"What's wrong?" she asked, hopping off the bed with Jeremy in her arms playing in her hair.

"Some shit is about to go down and I need to get to Montgomery ... like now," I told her as Fernando's phone went to voicemail.

As I tried reaching out to him again, I sloppily gathered my baby and my things. Beyond frustrated, I pondered where he was.

"Tell me what's going on, Zariah," Nene stated as she ran towards the vanity sink.

"I'll tell you the moment we get in the car," I replied as I dialed Gun'em's number.

On the fourth ring, he answered the phone. "What's up, Zariah?"

"Fernando's in danger. Dougie and some of the Burgundy niggas are going to set him—"

"Fuck!" he yelled before continuing, "He gon' to meet one of them niggas nih. Aye, I gotta go."

Dropping the luggage, I hollered, "Time to go now. Leave it. We'll come back for it."

My mind was all over the place as I placed my son into his car seat. He wasn't fully dressed like I would normally dress him, but I made sure to tuck a thin blanket over his body before throwing a heavier one over his car seat.

Finally out of the hotel room, we hustled to the rental car. I wasn't expecting the wind to be so brisk. If it wasn't for my determination to get to my man, I would've turned my ass around and nestled into the messy bed that had been my solace.

Once everyone was settled inside of the semi-warm car, I fled the hotel as I told Nene what Shardya said, followed by what Gun'em told me.

"Let me call Colby," she voiced while dialing his number.

Immediately, I began praying that I wouldn't have to bury my son's father, the love of my life. I wouldn't know what to do with myself if I couldn't see him every day.

With my phone in my hand, I called Gun'em. He didn't answer his phone.

"Colby, where are you?" Nene asked.

Shortly afterwards, she inquired, "Where are y'all going?"

"Okay. We are headed back to Montgomery. Me and the kids are going to your parents' home."

"You already know Zariah is not going to go to your parents' home, Colby. Not after the phone call she got from Shardya."

My girl knew me. Ever since Fernando and I had been dealing with each other, I had been his rider. I sure as hell wasn't going to stop now that his life was on the line. Just like he would move heaven for me, I would move it for him as well.

Looking at me, Nene said, "Colby and Gun'em said that you need to be at his parents' house with us."

"No can do. I'm going to make sure that Dougie and all them niggas will no longer breathe," I stated as I placed the hazard lights on and made the new model, white Hyundai Sonata do what it do—go fast.

After a couple more sentences with Colby, Nene ended the call. Planting her eyes on me as she gently rubbed my shaky hand, she stressed the importance of me not being in a hostile environment. I wasn't hearing any of that shit she was talking about.

I was glad when my cell phone rang. Quickly looking at my phone, an unknown number displayed. It was Shardya. Without a moment's hesitation, I answered the phone.

"He's here," she softly spoke as I overheard my brother talking to Fernando.

My heart sank as I began breathing slowly and deeply.

"Where are y'all?" I heard myself asking.

"At one of Daddy's homes in Sheridan Heights."

"Are they planning on taking him anywhere?"

"Yeah. To the abandoned building by the railroad tracks on the nawf side."

"How many of them are there?"

"Four."

"Where is Monia and Markesha?"

"They are out scouting for Colby and Gun'em."

Placing my phone on mute, I quickly told Nene to call Colby and tell them that Monia and Markesha was out looking for them.

"None of this shit is making any sense to me. Why are they so helping all of a sudden, Zariah? They ain't never helped you with shit before. Don't you find it odd that they are 'helping' now?"

"Yes, I do, but what can I do other than to halfway assist them. I don't know what else to do. What if she isn't lying? What if she's really doing the right thing?"

As Nene shrugged her shoulders, I unmuted my phone.

"They will be going to the abandoned building now. Bushmaster just pulled the black van in the backyard," she whispered before Dougie angrily shouted.

"Bitch, who yo' hoe-ish ass on the phone wit'?"

At that moment, I knew that Shardya wasn't on our brother's side. With that knowledge, I told Nene that she better get her feelings and mind right and get on the phone with Colby and Gun'em so that we could save my motherfucking man and my half of a sister!

Whatever it takes, my nigga coming out of this shit alive so that we can raise our son together.

Chapter Fifteen

Grinch

"We finally got yo' fuck ass nih," Dougie snarled as he gazed into my eyes.

"It seems that way, don't it?" I laughed while looking at the other scary ass niggas he had with him—the remaining members of the Burgundy crew.

"Shid, we gon' make you suffer before puttin' you in the ground, or should I say never to be found again," he voiced, stepping into my face.

"Then, my nigga handle yo' motherfuckin' business, do-boy."

One of the Burgundy nigga's phones rang, he silenced the call and nervously looked at Dougie.

"Why in the fuck are you lookin' at me like that, nigga?" Dougie spat briefly looking at the tall, light-skinned cat.

"No reason, Boss," the weakling stammered.

"Mane, this nigga here too scary. Why in the fuck you ain't killed him like you did som' of his folks?" I asked Dougie before laughing.

Underneath his breath, Dougie said, "Same thing I was thinkin'."

Without a moment's hesitation, Dougie gave that nigga a nice facial with a bullet from his .450 Bushmaster. Brains and skull matter flew onto the niggas that stood around the weakling. Happily growling, I was excited that Dougie fell into the palms of my hands by doing my dirty work.

"You should've been underneath us, Grinch. You have som' qualities that would've made this damn dynasty the truth. Why you never committed to being underneath the Price Dynasty?" Dougie inquired as he glared at the dead body.

"Because I liked workin' within a small knit crew. Y'all stay in the limelight when it comes down to the police, an' that wasn't my steelo. Y'all niggas too greedy fo' me. I ain't wit' that prison shit, an' I sure as hell ain't wit' shootin' fo' the fuck of it. Basically, the Price Dynasty is a catastrophe," I replied as I pulled out a cigarette and fired it up.

"Dougie, why this motherfuckin' nigga ain't tied up?" Bushmaster loudly questioned from the back door of the multi-family home.

Bushmaster was another child of Nathan; he was one of Nathan's muscle men. That six foot two, dread head, gold-teeth, buff, dark-skinned nigga got his name from one of the best rifles that he loved shooting.

Instead of responding to his brother, Dougie shouted, "Bitch, who yo' hoe-ish ass on the phone wit'?"

Turning my head in the direction he was looking at, I saw Shardya crouched low in the hallway with a flip phone pressed to her ear.

As she closed the phone, she said, "No ... nobody boy and I got yo' hoe ... fuck boy!"

Snatching his sister off the ground, Dougie shoved the nozzle of the rifle underneath her chin and grabbed her pussy.

Oh my fuckin' Jesus. What kind of shit is this?

"It's yo' turn, Shardya. I heard how you be fuckin' these niggas. I wanna see what you 'bout. I love seein' how good the products be. So, you know what you need to do, right?" Dougie evilly questioned as he unbuttoned his sister's pants.

What kind of fuckery am I lookin' at?

Her body grew rigid as her eyes bucked from their small sockets. With a nasty look on his ugly face, Dougie stuck his hand into his sister's pants. Shit had gone too far, and I refused to let it go any further. It was apparent that Shardya was scared and extremely disgusted.

Not the one to witness the fuckery of incest rape, I cleared my throat and said, "Aye, nigga, ain't you finna kill me or som'? After all, I did knock yo' daddy off."

By the motion of his hand and the helpless soft cry from Shardya's tightly closed mouth, I knew that Dougie stuck his fingers inside of his sister's core. My stomach flipped as he told her that he was going to shove his dick inside of her like he did Monia and Markesha.

I gotta stop this shit. Som' kind of way I gotta stop this shit. God, let Zariah know how much I love her an' our son an' that I never wanted anythin' of this nature to happen, I thought before I nastily said, "Mane, brang yo' sick ass on over here an' kill the motherfucka that slaughtered yo' daddy an' cruised away without a care in the world."

My comment ceased him from his nasty actions. As he removed the gun away from her face, he slowly pulled his hand out of her pants. Shardya was shaking as tears slid down her pretty face. Glaring at his sister, Dougie stuck two fingers into his mouth and sucked on them. Instantly, I began gagging. My damn stomach wasn't right at all.

"I can't wait to spread yo' motherfuckin' legs an' taste every ounce of you. Monia an' Markesha really gonna have a reason to hate yo' sexy ass. I'mma eat yo' ass into a coma," he stated before snatching the flip phone out of her shaky hand.

"Mane, brang yo' ass on!" I angrily yelled.

"Damn nigga, you eager to die, ain't it?" He laughed, strolling towards me.

"Hell yes. I ain't wit' this nasty shit you got going on. Nigga, that's yo' motherfuckin' sister! I don't give a fuck if she got a different mother than you ... she still yo' blood, nigga."

Chuckling as he fired up a cigarette, that creep ass nigga said, "Shid, who said we got the same momma, nigga? Tha fuck you mean."

Right then, I knew that nigga was nowhere near sane. I glared at him as if I was the dumb one. I couldn't believe the shit that he said and did. He had to go. If he was raping his sisters, he would be after Zariah and that right there would cause me to end their entire fucking bloodline, down to the kids.

"Time to go," Bushmaster voiced sternly.

"Welp, I guess you finna meet yo' maker nih, Grinch," Dougie quickly voiced as he held out the blunt to me.

Shaking my head, I said, "I'm good on that tip."

"What, you don't like a dirty blunt?" he asked as he placed the nozzle of the rifle into my back and nudged it—indicating for me to move towards the door.

"Hell nawl, my nigga, that ain't my steelo. You can have that shit to yo' self."

When we made it to the door, Dougie said, "Snatch Shardya's ass up."

"Nawl, bruh, we need to take care of this nigga," Bushmaster voiced sternly.

"Did you not hear what the fuck I said?" Dougie loudly yelled, turning around to look at his baby brother.

"An' nigga did you hear what the fuck I said?" Bushmaster piped back with much attitude as he clung onto his weapon.

"The throne is mine nih, thanks to Grinch doing me a favor. So, I suggest if you want to continue breathin' ... you better do what the fuck I say."

Chuckling, Bushmaster stepped to his brother and spoke through clenched teeth, "You ain't stupid enough to end me, my nigga. Like I motherfuckin' said, she ain't goin' no damn where. We finna—"

From outside, shots rang out, slamming inside of the house. Jumping into survival mode, I dropped low and popped Dougie in the stomach. As vomit flew out of his mouth on to the floor and me, I caught his gun and began making my way out of the war zone.

Déjà vu.

Chaos was at an all-time high as bullets knocked holes into the walls, shattered glass, and ripped through one of those goofy ass niggas. Making my way down the hallway, I prayed that a bullet didn't catch me in my side again. That was the last thing that I needed. As I ducked off into a room away from the street, I saw Shardya climbing out of a window.

In a flash, I was through the window, running like a bat from a cave with Dougie's rifle in my hand. As Shardya jumped a fence, the shots continued. I prayed that my niggas from Selma slaughtered everyone in the house, just like I told them to do.

In a safe range away from the chaos, Shardya stopped running and began walking. I hollered her name, and she kept moving.

"Aye!" I hollered behind her as people stood on their porches chatting amongst themselves and looking at us.

Shardya kept walking with her head down. I knew her mind was on what happened prior to the shootout. I was very sure that she didn't want me in her presence. Yet, I had to make sure that she was okay.

Jogging behind her, I called her name.

Turning around to face me, she angrily asked, "What in the fuck do you want, Grinch?"

Before I could respond, I heard the police sirens wailing as a familiar faced young nigga hollered, "Aye, Grinch ... y'all post up ova here. The block finna be hot as fuck."

"A'ight," I told him as I grabbed Shardya's arm and pulled her towards a red, brick home.

As I stepped on the property of God knows who, I greeted those that were outside staring at us. The siren wailed closer to us and the young dude opened the door to an old school beat up Delta '88. Shoving the rifle in the backseat, I looked at Shardya and asked her if I could talk to her for a minute.

"No, Grinch, I don't want to talk," she voiced softly not looking at me.

"I'm not going to ask a-motherfuckin'-gain," I growled in a low tone.

Sighing heavily, she nodded her head and stepped away from the small crowd that surrounded us.

Clearing my throat, I looked at the young dude and said, "I'm finna step off an' chat wit' her fo' a minute. Then, I will come back an' break you off som' som' fo' lookin' out."

"Nawl, fam, you good."

"You sure?"

"Hell yeah. You Gucci in my eyes. Shid, if it wasn't fo' you, then I wouldn't be alive today."

With a strange look on my face, I glared into the light-skinned dude's face that held a scar underneath his right eye. Within minutes, I knew who the little dude was.

Quickly, I held out my hand as I had a smile on my face. "Mane, I wondered fo' the longest how you was doing. You good?"

"Yeah. I ain't tryin' to gangbang no mo' or be out in these streets. I'm back in school an' workin' part time."

"I'm glad you listened to what I said," I told him as a loud mouth woman showed her ass.

"That nigga Grinch need to get the hell off this property before the police be all up and in this damn house. The last thing I need is fo' those funky ass cops to be harrassin' us."

"Ma, calm down," the young one stated.

"Get yo' ass in this damn house, Darnell," the woman yelled.

"But Ma—"

"Just do what she say ... she is right," I told him before I held out my balled fist.

He didn't get a chance to dap me up because his mother was in my face talking cash money shit.

Rubbing my beard, I glared at the woman while nodding my head. I couldn't object to anything that she said because she was telling the truth. Right now, I was too hot for anyone to be around me. It was no secret that I placed a war in the streets.

"Ma, you doin' all that cappin'. If it wasn't fo' Grinch, you wouldn't have me today. He was shot because I fell an' broke my ankle. That bullet would've took me out the game. So, you poppin' off at the wrong one," Darnell said while looking at his mother.

Immediately, the woman stopped talking and looked at me with apologetic eyes.

She opened her mouth to say something, but I shook my head and said, "You don't have to say anything. Honestly, it's best that you don't. As soon as them folks get out of the neighborhood, I'mma leave. Right now, it's too hot fo' me to move wit' a stick."

Going against what I told her, the woman spoke anyway. "I'm sorry for how I've acted. Every day, it's a shootout in these streets. Every day, someone is getting a call about their loved one. If I had've known that you saved my son, I would've never stepped to you in that manner. I thank God every day for my son being alive, and I should start thanking you every day as well."

As I nodded my head, she gave me a hug and thanked me repeatedly.

Shortly afterwards, she pulled away from me and said, "So, you are the one that left him with an important message before you passed out?"

"I am."

With tears in her eyes, she placed her chunky hand over her mouth and cried. Knowing exactly what I told him and what I would tell Jeremy when he got older, I looked towards the sky so that the tears that were on the verge of dropping would not escape my eyes. Counting to twenty, I dropped my head and looked Darnell in the face.

"You make sure you remember what I told you, and you pass that information on to yo' kids ... one day," I told him seriously while someone yelled that a coroner van had pulled up to Nathan's home.

I hope the coroner van is going to hold every single body that I had the displeasure of being around within the last thirty damn minutes, I thought as I placed my eyes on Shardya.

Moving away from Darnell and his mother, I didn't know what I was going to say to her, but I knew that I had to say something.

"Aye, you okay?" I asked in a low tone.

Shaking her head, she softly replied, "Not really."

"Do you want to talk 'bout it?"

"I'm not sure that I should ... it seems surreal. I ... I..." she stammered, looking at the ground.

"Is anyone else like that besides him?"

She nodded her head.

"Do they ... um ... hurt you or make you do things against yo' will?" I struggled to ask.

I prayed that she said no. It took her a while to answer; thus, I knew the answer.

"Bushmaster?" I whispered.

With tears dripping down her face, she nodded her head.

"Have y'all told anyone?"

"An' that shit didn't turn out well. Father overheard Dougie doing it to Monia an' he damn near killed her. He refused to chastise Dougie. Father just let him do whatever the fuck he wanted. So, I didn't see a reason to open my mouth. Markesha didn't say anything either."

"Damn it, y'all could have told somebody," I growled angrily.

"Who was going to believe us? Nathan Price's daughters ... the ones he trained to scheme, frame, and seduce niggas into workin' underneath him. The entire law enforcement looks at us as if we are a piece of shit. There wouldn't be a knight in shining armor to protect us like you protect Zariah. We didn't have the luxury of having a maternal grandmother that cared for us. My great, great, great, great grandmother built the Price Dynasty; she was beyond corrupt and enforced that everyone in the family be a criminals as well. That damn woman is the reason why the Prices are thrown the fuck off."

I was at a loss of words. There wasn't anything that I could say to Shardya; thus, I pulled her into my arms. All this time, I thought negatively of Monia, Markesha, and Shardya and didn't know the hell they were going through with their brothers and father. I was highly thankful that Zariah didn't go around them; she would be beyond mentally messed up. The thought of those sick bastards touching Zariah put me in a headspace that caused me to think about destroying the Price Dynasty for their wicked ways.

"Aye, Man Man, may I use yo' phone?" Shardya asked a short, dark-skinned guy with a low haircut.

"Yeah," he replied as he waltzed towards us. "You good?"

Nodding her head, she responded, "Yeah."

Placing his phone into her hand, Shardya softly said, "Thank you."

"No problem."

As he stepped a few inches away from us, I checked out the scene and paid attention to the gossip that was spilling out of people's mouths.

"He's safe," Shardya stated into the phone.

Her comment took me away from the observation of the streets.

"Yeah. We on Bowman Lane," she continued in the phone.

"We are in the yard that is filled with people."

With a raised eyebrow, I wondered who she was talking to. In less than one minute, I knew.

"Your lady wants to talk to you," Shardya announced.

I had so many questions for Shardya, but I had to wait until after I talked to Zariah.

"Hello."

"Hey, are you okay?" my woman questioned before sighing.

"Yes, I'm fine. Where are you?"

"Coming out of Chilton County. Nene on the phone with Colby and Gun'em. They are on the way to get you."

"Okay. I love you, Zariah," I replied as I saw Gun'em's truck creeping down the road.

"I love you more, Fernando," she cooed.

"I'll call you once I get in the truck wit' Gun'em an' Colby," I told her as I moved towards the old school car to retrieve the rifle.

"Make sure that you do so."

"I will."

Before I ended the call, I blew a kiss into the phone. With the rifle in my hand, I gave Shardya the phone to hand back to ole boy. Gun'em and Colby hopped out of the truck and greeted folks in the yard.

"Damn, boy, you stay in som' shit, don't it?" Colby jokingly questioned as we dapped each other up.

"Hell yeah," I replied as Gun'em and I dapped each other up.

"Shid, let's blow this hot ass spot," they announced in unison.

"Shid, I'm wit' that," I told them as I held out my hand for Shardya to place her hand in mine.

Shaking her head, she said, "Nawl, Grinch. Your protection stops here. I'm good. Thank you so much."

Growling, I sternly said, "Guh, put yo' fuckin' hand in mine an' let's go."

"I'on want nobody to think that you and me fuckin'."

"I'on give a fuck what nobody thinks. You of all people should know that, Shardya. Fuck these folks an' let's go. That's an order!" I barked.

Shaking her head with a little smile on her face, she said, "Now, I see why my sister won't let you go. Oh, ugly bossy ass, Grinch."

"Now, what in the hell did we miss between the two of y'all?" Gun'em inquired with a raised eyebrow.

Shardya and I looked at each other before she softly said, "He's not a surly Grinch after all."

As we skipped towards Gun'em's truck, I wondered who died in the house.

The moment we hopped inside and sped off, I asked, "Who's dead?"

"From what the witnesses are sayin', everyone in the house is dead," Colby replied as he fired up a cigarette.

"Wonderful news," I spoke as a sigh of relief exited my mouth.

I grabbed Shardya's hand, squeezed it, and said, "Are you sure that you, Monia, an' Markesha free from the fuckery?"

As tears cascaded down her pretty face, she nodded her head and said, "Yes, we are."

I had to make sure; thus, I asked again, "Are you absolutely sure that y'all are free?"

"Yes, Grin—"

She stopped her sentence and began shaking, uncontrollably.

"What's wrong?" I asked in a worried tone.

"I just saw Bushmaster," she voiced in a scared tone.

"Where?" Colby, Gun'em, and I asked in unison.

She didn't get a chance to respond before we saw him. I asked for Colby's phone.

The moment he placed it into my hand, I told Sharyda, "I need you to get in contact wit' Monia an' Markesha. I'mma get y'all to a safe spot. I gotta knock this nigga off."

"Cuz, you gotta explain som' shit to me nih," Colby said as he turned around to look at me.

"All you need to know is that I gotta kill Bushmaster tonight," I told him as I glared at the fuck nigga before Gun'em turned off the street.

I won't sleep well knowin' that this nasty ass nigga is on the streets rapin' his sister.

Chapter Sixteen

Zariah

Christmas Eve

There was so much drama that we couldn't focus on the holiday season, but we tried our best to put our lives back together the best that we could. Once I returned from Birmingham, we stayed at Fernando's house and so did Gun'em, Colby, Nene, Monia, Markesha, and Shardya. Immediately, I was against my sisters staying. I voiced my opinion and Fernando told me not to question anything that he said. From that day until three days ago, we argued about them being in the same house as us.

Even though my man and I argued about my sisters staying in his home, new bonds and memories were created. Everyone forgave each other for the things that happened, as children and adults. Nanna, Colby Senior, Maryann, Colby Junior, and Fernando had a long talk eight days ago. Colby Junior and Nene had their talk as well as Fernando and me.

Jeremy officially met his aunts, and he was in love with Shardya more so than the other two. My son had a lot to say in baby language as he gazed into her almond-shaped, light-brown eyes. I thought it was the cutest thing in the world. Seeing them interact with each other caused me to stop worrying about them being so close to my man; after all, it was the time of year where family came together and showered each other with love and appreciation.

"Who told y'all to do all this shoppin'?" Fernando, Gun'em, and Colby asked in an annoyed tone as they stepped through the cabin's door.

The fellas and the elders thought it was best to spend Christmas through New Years' Day in a cabin located in Mentone, Alabama. Of course, I was against it, but I was outnumbered; thus, I had to deal with it.

Laughing, Nene said, "Stop all that damn complainin' an' get them in here, so we can wrap them up."

"Y'all had shit stuffed everywhere. When did y'all have time to shop?" Fernando inquired as Gun'em walked towards Shardya and kneeled in front of her.

With my eyes on them, I said, "You can shop from online from anywhere, sir."

"You okay?" Gun'em softly asked Shardya.

Nodding her head, she said, "Yeah."

"Yo' ass been sayin' yeah since you hopped in my truck nine days ago. I want you to be honest wit' me. Are you okay?" Gun'em questioned again, grabbing her shaky hand.

Stepping from the back of the cabin, Monia looked towards Shardya and said, "Um, Shardya, I need to talk to you ... Markesha, you need to be present as well."

Instantly, I was pissed off. How dare she not include Nene and me? Monia and Markesha were distant as it was. If it wasn't for the guys asking them questions, they wouldn't say shit. I was eager to understand why they didn't want to say shit to Nene and me; hell, we made sure that we included them in everything!

"Um, what's up with y'all two, Monia and Markesha, not including or barely talking to Nene and me? Hell, we are doing everything to accommodate y'all asses and y'all wanna act stank than a mother—"

Fernando loudly and sternly said, "Zariah, don't do that shit. Not today! Calm down, mane."

Standing to my feet, I said, "I know motherfucking well you ain't talking to me in that manner, nigga. I know damn well you ain't taking up for them."

"Zariah, all I'm sayin' is calm down an' don't start no shit," he voiced in a tone that made me sit my ass down.

Angry as hell, I looked at Monia and Markesha as Shardya slowly walked passed me. I couldn't understand why my man was so protective over the bitches that made my life a living hell right along with our funky ass family.

Christmas music played in the background as Nene rubbed my arm and said, "They'll be out of here within an hour or two. All we gotta do is make them feel uncomfortable, and Grinch will have them gone."

"He better or I will disappear," I voiced in a nasty manner as Shardya reappeared with a pale, horrified facial expression.

"What's wrong?" the fellas asked, looking at her.

"Look at this dramatic shit here," Nene whispered in my ear.

Shaking her head, Shardya replied, "Nothing. I need some air. Alone."

"Nawl, you ain't allowed to be by yo'self. That was the deal, remember?" Fernando voiced sternly as he stood in her face.

Instantly, I hopped to my feet and yelled, "One of y'all motherfuckers is going to tell me what in the fuck is up or it's gonna be some furniture moving in this bitch!"

"Grinch, Colby, and Gun'em, we appreciate y'all helping us and all, but we should be going," Markesha stated in an odd tone.

I pointed at her and said, "I agree with that."

"Zariah, sit yo' ass down. Markesha, y'all ain't going no-damn-where 'til I get confirmation that Bushmaster is dead," Fernando stated with an ugly expression plastered across his face.

"I ain't sitting down until you tell me what is really goin—"

Looking at me with a sad expression as tears dripped down her face, Shardya's voice shook as she said, "Dougie was raping Monia and Markesha. He wanted me next. The day of the shooting he stuck his hands in my pants in front of Grinch. Grinch's crazy ass said some shit to stop the unwanted things he was doing to me. Bushmaster has been doing unwanted things to me for as long as I can remember. I ... I just learned that I'm pregnant ... Bushmaster ... my fucking blood brother's kid. Grinch sent out an order to have Bushmaster killed. Once he's dead, my sisters and I will be out of y'all hair ... for good."

"Oh, my God," Nene spoke into her hand.

My mouth was on the floor as my heart sunk to my ass. My knees grew weak as Shardya, Monia, and Markesha passed me with their heads low.

"Every time I think about what that fuck nigga did to his sister, I want his fuckin' head," Gun'em voiced as he aggressively walked passed me.

As I took a seat, Fernando looked at me and said, "Now you see why I have them so close to me? You are just as much Bushmaster's sister as they are. I couldn't leave them knowing what they had endured an' would continue to endure while he's still alive. This type of attention an' love is foreign to them. They didn't have anyone to care fo' them like you had Nanna to take you away from the bullshit. Nathan caught Dougie doing shit to Monia an' almost beat her to death. So, he condoned the shit."

"You saw what Dougie was doing to Shardya?" Nene inquired in disbelief.

"Yep. Damn guh was scared as shit. I thought Bushmaster was savin' her when he told Dougie that Shardya wasn't going wit' us to the warehouse, but that nigga wasn't savin' her. He didn't want Dougie or anyone else to know that Shardya had been marked by him already."

The sliding door to the back porch of the cabin opened and in walked Monia and Markesha with tears dripping down their faces. I stood with an apologetic facial expression. I had some things to say to them, but nothing left my mouth. I just stared at them.

"You don't have to look at us like that. We were just less fortunate than you. We are still human, Zariah," Monia sadly voiced as she looked at Grinch and said, "We are really uncomfortable now that Shardya decided to tell our darkest, nastiest secret. Can you please take us back to Montgomery?"

"No," Fernando said.

"Please," they begged.

"Why?"

"It's embarrassing being here. I just want to go home an' deal wit' this shit the best way that I can. It is what it is," Monia voiced as she fumbled with her hands.

"You ain't leavin', damn it! I'mma protect you! I can't just ride back wit' Grinch to drop you off in that hellhole! I told you that day that I would protect you an' I meant that shit!" Gun'em stated loudly from the back porch.

Turning to look in his direction, I saw him snatch Shardya into his arms as they descended towards the ground. As Gun'em cradled my sister, Monia and Markesha walked towards the back of the cabin. Nene and I were on their heels. Once inside of the room, they sunk to the floor and cried into their hands.

Looking at the ceiling, I closed my eyes and prayed for them. The pain that they felt would've been my pain if Nanna hadn't gotten custody of me. I would be in their shoes as we speak, suffering from years of abuse with no love or guidance.

"You wanna know how we survived the shit?" Markesha asked as she wiped the tears away and stood.

Slowly, I nodded my head.

"At first, we got high from the time we woke up until we went to sleep. Then, we added alcohol in our lives."

Outside, we heard Maryann, Colby Senior, and Nanna chuckling. Within a matter of seconds, Shardya and Gun'em stepped into the room.

"I hate to ask this, but Monia an' Markesha, is there a chance that y'all are pregnant, too?" Gun'em voiced in an awkward tone.

Markesha shook her head; whereas, Monia nodded hers.

"Fuck," he said as Nene and I dropped our shaking heads.

"How late, Monia?"

"A week and some days," she softly replied as the elders stepped into the home, inquiring about us.

"Um, um …," he stated as the door opened.

"What's wrong?" Fernando and Colby inquired in unison with a raised eyebrow.

"Okay, fellas, it's time for y'all to leave. Nene and I got this from here," I stated while looking each of them in the eyes.

"Not 'til you tell us what's wrong," my bossy ass man said.

"It's okay, you can tell him, Zariah," Monia announced.

Sighing heavily, I said, "Monia may be pregnant also."

"Them fuck ass niggas," Colby spoke through clenched teeth.

"What do you need me to do, Monia an' Shardya?" Fernando inquired.

"Nothing. We can take care of it."

"Elaborate," he said.

"Once the holidays are over, we are going to have an abortion."

We were stuck in a delicate, complex situation; thus, we tried to handle it the best that we could. Not a soul knew what to say, including me. Time past before the fellas left the room. Shortly after they left, Nanna stepped into the room.

"Monia, Shardya, and Markesha," she said, inches away from them.

"Ma'am," they replied.

"Everything that y'all have endured will make y'all stronger and wiser. When y'all mother passed away, I thought y'all were going into the hands of wonderful people. I was sadly mistaken the moment they didn't step up to take *all* y'all away from your father's family. They tried, sweethearts, but of course the State of Alabama failed you three, Dougie, and Bushmaster. Nathan's money and his last name moved mountains so that y'all would forever be in his custody. I'm so sorry y'all had to endure being raised by that creature," she softly said as they embraced.

At that moment, I wondered whether Nanna knew what Dougie and Bushmaster had done to them. When she exited the room, I was on her heels.

Softly calling her name, she turned around to face me.

"Yes, dear?"

"What else do you know ... about them?"

"I rather not disclose that information."

Whispering, I asked, "Does it have to do with Dougie doing unbrotherly things to Monia and Markesha, as Bushmaster did to Shardya?"

When my grandmother nodded her head, my knees gave out. She caught me and whispered in my ear, "Jovan touching you ... down there ... was the reason why I sought custody of you."

With a horrid look on my face, I glared at my grandmother as I processed the information that she dropped on me. I couldn't believe that Bushmaster touched me.

Thus, I shrieked, "What?" and continued, "But, Nanna I was young when you became my guardian. What do you mean he touched me?"

"You know exactly what I mean, baby," she softly stated as she rubbed my face.

"He did me like he did Shardya, minus the pregnant part?" I asked as my vision became blurry.

She nodded her head before pulling me into her arms. The floodgates opened as I cried.

"I wanted to kill him, but Jovan was just ten-years-old. That day, I kept you in my custody. I refused to let you go. I told Nathan of his son's behavior, and that bastard laughed and sent me on my merry way with a nice message saying that he didn't give a damn what his boys did to girls that was only good for one thing."

A door opened, and I heard my sisters and Nene ask, "Zariah, are you okay?"

Gently holding onto my face, Nanna said, "It's time for you and your sisters to bond, together and privately."

Nodding my head, I said, "Okay."

As we stood, Nanna looked at Nene and said, "Dear, they need some time together. Would you like to assist an old lady on a dating website?"

"Oh wow," Nene voiced before chuckling and skipping away with my grandmother.

Biting my bottom lip to keep me from crying, I lowly said, "Bushmaster touched me also."

***

"Today has been eventful, huh?" Fernando said as he sat on the bed, pulling me close to him.

"More eventful than you know," I replied in a blank tone, glaring at the ceiling.

"You mad at me?" he asked, turning my head so that I could look at him.

"No."

"Are you lying to me?"

"Have I ever?"

"Not that I can recall."

"Okay, then."

"What's up wit' this dry tone?"

"Just thinking. Sorry for the tone," I told him as I placed a kiss on his side.

"What are you thinkin' 'bout? Your sisters an' what they have endured?"

Nodding my head, I replied, "Yeah."

"Sit up so I can hold you."

I did as he told me. Even though I was in the arms of the one that I'd always loved and showered me with so much adoration, my body felt foreign against his. I tried to shake the things that Nanna told me, but I couldn't. I vowed that I wouldn't tell Fernando, but I felt as if he needed to know. I was never good at keeping things away from him.

"Fernando," I softly said as I looked into his loving face.

"What's up, beautiful?"

Sighing heavily, I said, "Bushmaster touched me when I was younger. Nanna told me today after y'all left the room. She knew about his ways. She told Nathan about it, and he said some nasty shit."

"Zariah, please tell me you didn't just say what I think you said," he stated through clenched teeth while glaring at me with hurt filled eyes.

"He took my innocence, baby," I heard myself say before crying.

As he tightly held me, rocking back and forth, his cell phone rang.

Clearing his throat, he answered it. "Tell me somethin' good ... like right fuckin' nih."

Shortly afterwards, he spat, "We are on the way."

Ending the call, Fernando said, "Zariah, the fellas an' I finna go handle this nigga Bushmaster. I'll be back the moment I cease him from breathin'."

"Don't leave me. Have them do it, please," I cried, holding onto him tighter.

"Zariah, I want to kill this nigga my-motherfuckin'-self. I will be back before you know it. I promise. You can get a full night sleep since Nanna has Jeremy. Baby, you need the rest."

Nanna thought it was best that Jeremy slept in the room with her, and I didn't disagree with her.

Seven minutes later, Colby, Gun'em, and Fernando were gone and the ladies were in the bed with me. We didn't talk about anything that we had learned, or why the fellas left at eleven o'clock at night. As we listened to music, each of us was in a world of our own. We tried to be happy and sane, but it was hard doing so.

"Okay, I know if I'm tired of thinking about today's events ... I know y'all are. Can we please play cards, dance, or do something other than sulk around?" Nene asked.

"Damn, Nene, it took yo' ass long enough to say somethin' of this nature." Markesha snickered.

The fun began, and I was thankful for it. When the fellas returned, we were amped and ready for them to join in on the fun. However, it didn't go as planned. Colby ran to Nene, Gun'em ran to Monia, Markesha, and Shardya, and Fernando ran to me.

"What's wrong?" we asked in a worried tone.

They didn't say a word as they hugged us tight.

Shortly afterwards, Gun'em and Fernando replied, "He's dead, an' we made sure that the rest of Nathan's sons won't fuck wit' y'all."

"What exactly did y'all do?" I inquired, pulling away from Fernando.

"What needed to be done, so don't ask no mo'," he voiced with a raised eyebrow.

"Nene, I think it's time fo' us to retire to bed," Colby said as he lifted her up.

She nodded her head and told us goodnight.

"Night," we replied.

"Y'all can hangout wit' me if y'all wanna ... I'm finna play the game though," Gun'em told my sisters.

"Shid, I got first dibs on the game," Shardya spoke before laughing.

"Cool." He smiled before continuing, "I'mma tell y'all ret nih, Zariah, Monia an' Markesha ... when I get my head an' feelin's in check, y'all gonna be my sista-in-laws ... if an' when Shardya deems *we* are ready."

Thrown off by his comment, I opened my mouth and said, "Before you think you are going to skip out of this damn room, you got some questions to answer."

"Um, after the shooting at Best Buy, I made it my business to check on Gun'em every day," my sister replied with a small smile on her face.

With a shocked facial expression, I said, "Ooh."

"I hate to be rude, but y'all asses got to get out of here," Fernando softly said before chuckling.

After we said goodnight to each other, my man and I were alone, glaring into each other faces. Our body language spoke volumes.

With tears in his eyes, Fernando sweetly asked, "May I touch you, MaZariah Chloe Nash?"

Knowing why he looked the way he did and why he asked me that question, I said, "You will never look at me this way again, and you shall never ask me that question. Understood?"

Pulling me into his arms, he cried as he apologized for something that he didn't do nor that either of us knew about. I had to cease his heartbreak and tears. He was not going to feel as if he failed me when he didn't.

"I chopped that nigga into pieces, baby. I set that bastard's body parts on fire. He was a foul ass nigga fo' the shit he did to you an' Sharyda. Y'all will never be approached by any of the Prices' again … we made fuckin' sure of that. Do you hear me?" Fernando said as I wiped his tears away.

Nodding my head, I said, "Yes, baby, I hear you."

"I wanna make love to you," he groaned as he took my shirt off.

"Then, let's do so," I replied as I unbuckled his belt and pants.

From the moment he gently pushed me back on the bed, took off my pants, spread my legs, and French-kissed my kitty, tears seeped down my face as I repeatedly told him that I loved him and that I was going to forever love him.

My Fernando. My Grinch.

Chapter Seventeen

Grinch

Christmas

Today was the day that I felt should be the new beginning for everyone. Today was the day that everyone could breathe easier and live life with those that would have our backs and love us unconditionally. I wasn't going to allow negative past events to outshine this day, which was supposed to be filled with love, joy, smiles, and full bellies.

When I decided to have half of the unruly males in the Price Dynasty murdered, I did so with thoughts of Zariah, Shardya, Monia, and Markesha in mind. The moment the deed was complete, a huge weight lifted off my shoulders and for the first time in months, I truly felt free from the streets. That was something that Zariah had begged and prayed for. She deserved to live stress free from the lifestyle I brought her way.

"So, you just ain't gonna go to sleep, huh?" she asked before yawning.

With a smile on my face as I shook my head, I replied, "Merry Christmas, woman."

Giggling like a schoolgirl, she said, "Oops, I sort of forgot what today is. Merry Christmas, baby. I love you."

"I love you the most," I told her as the sun began to rise.

Snuggling further into me, Zariah rested her head on my chest and said, "I'm sleepy, baby."

"You should be." I laughed and continued, "All that nuttin' you did on a nigga's dick an' mouth."

"Oou, don't even talk 'bout it before I tell you to make me nut again." She chuckled.

With a raised eyebrow, I snatched the covers off her and spread her legs.

"I was just play—"

The slow flickers of my tongue across her pink bud ceased her from continuing with her statement. My baby's legs started shaking as she arched her back. Her juices gushed out of her as I made sounds to inform her just how tasty she was.

"Fernandooo, you need to stop," she moaned, gripping the back of my head.

"Why?" I asked, snaking two fingers inside of her as the once quiet cabin was full of cheerful greetings.

"Merry Christmas from Colby, nucca!" my foolish ass cousin spat as he busted into the room.

Zariah scrambled for the covers as I pushed her back and lay on top of her.

"Colby, get out of the room!" I laughed.

Childishly speaking, that fool said, "Oou, y'all so nasty! I'm finna tell!"

"Boy, get your childish ass out of that damn room. I bet you got an eye full," Auntie Maryann stated while laughing, causing everyone to laugh as well.

When the door closed behind us, I said, "You can bet we gonna finish this later."

Hopping out of the bed, I popped Zariah on the behind. Giggling, we put on our clothes and walked into the bathroom. While taking a shower, I was tempted to bend Zariah over and give him some great shower loving; however, the elders were calling our names.

Fifteen minutes later, Zariah joined the ladies in the kitchen. I stepped on the back porch with the fellas. As we smoked and talked, I was surprised when Uncle Colby told us that he wanted to hit the blunt.

With a surprised look on his face Colby asked, "So, nih you wanna smoke the green?"

"Dealing with you three, how in the fuck did you think I stayed sane?" He laughed.

Handing him the blunt, Gun'em said, "Oou, smoke it. We a handful."

Clearing my throat while briefly looking into the cabin, I asked Colby, "You got that fo' me?"

"An' you know I do," he replied as he handed me the small, gray box.

Gun'em and Uncle Colby had a grin on their faces as Gun'em said, "My nigga."

"I'm finally ready nih."

"Your cousin should be right behind you. He steady poppin' babies in Nene ... his ass should gon' head and snatch her off the market also," Uncle Colby stated as he passed me the blunt.

Wiping out a pink box, Colby smile and said, "Daddy ain't raise no full blown fool nih!"

"Null, nih!" we said in unison.

"Y'all crazy if y'all think I'mma let another nigga get my queen."

"Cornell, it—"

"Dude, you ain't changed yo' name yet? No wonder you have them guhs call you Gun'em. You got an old man name," Colby said as I laughed.

Laughing, Gun'em stated, "Oou, Colby Senior, that's why I don't deal wit' you on that tip. You like to call folks by their government name."

"Yep," my high ass uncle replied as he stood and continued, "Now, we gotta get you a woman so you can settle down."

As he nodded his head, our laughter died. Seeing the look on his face, I knew it was time for us to take things seriously.

"He lost a special someone at the shootin' that took place in Best Buy, Uncle Colby. It's gon' take him a minute to get his mind right," I said as I took a seat beside my partner.

"Shid, I highly doubt that. Not the way that he's been hovering around Shardya ... catering to her every need and holding her while she's asleep," my uncle voiced.

"Once our minds are right, I'll be Cornell fo' her," he spoke softly, sitting back into the wooden chair as he looked into the cabin.

At that moment, we embraced in a manly hug as Uncle Colby said, "Thank you Jesus for answering my prayers."

Colbon's voice broke up our manly bonding time. "It's time to eat."

Without a moment's hesitation, we filed into the cabin. The delicious smelling food caused my mouth to water. I was eager to eat as I took Jeremy out of the swinger. Placing several kisses on my son's forehead, I looked around the dining area of the cabin and smiled. I was amazed at the love that flowed amongst us. If I was a soft ass nigga, I would've cried in front of the ladies as they placed plates filled with food on the beautiful, large, circular, oak table.

Once we sat at the table, Uncle Colby said grace. The moment he finished blessing the food and praying over us, we ate and talked. Zariah and I took turns feeding Jeremy food off our plates. Our greedy son became angry whenever we fed ourselves; thus, I told my baby to eat her food and I would feed him mine.

"When can we open our presents?" Colbon asked.

"Soon as we are done eating," Auntie Maryann replied.

"Y'all need to hurry up and eat. I'm ready to see what I got," he excitedly stated, causing us to laugh.

Thirty minutes later, the table was clean, and we sat in the living room watching Colbon open his gifts. Everything he wanted, he received. The look on his face was priceless when he opened a small box and held out a pair of booties.

"I'm going to be a big brother?" he asked with the biggest grin.

"Yep," we replied in unison.

He ran towards his parents and said, "Oou, now I get to boss someone around like Grinch does you, Daddy."

As I laughed, I said, "Nawl, Colbon, it's the other way 'round ... yo' daddy be bossin' me 'round."

"Either way, I'm bossin' somebody 'round ... I can see it now," he replied as he lifted his head towards the ceiling while tapping on his lips.

"Boy, if you don't stop." Nene chuckled.

Right before the gifts from underneath the tree were gone, Gun'em, Colby, and I slipped outside to his truck and gathered the gifts that we purchased for Monia, Markesha, and Shardya; Gun'em was supposed to have placed them underneath the tree, but apparently his ass was occupied holding Shardya and forgot about the gifts.

"Are y'all serious?" Nene asked curiously as Shardya stepped from the back with a pretty Christmas bag.

"We didn't want to leave Monia, Markesha, and Shardya out, so yesterday we decided to get them something as well," Colby announced as he handed Monia a large gift bag.

"Aww," everyone said happily as I handed Markesha her bag.

Gun'em handed Shardya the gift bag and nervously said, "Merry Christmas, Shardya."

With a smile on her face, she said, "Merry Christmas, Cornell, and thank you."

"Hot-got-damn! She called him by his government name! Oou, the Lord answered all my prayers ... well, minus two!" my auntie happily shouted while standing and clapping her hands.

As we laughed and showered each other with warm words and love, I cleared my throat and told Colby that I had to speak with him.

Disappearing into the room he shared with Nene and Colbon, I said, "Mane, I need yo' help."

"Wit' what?"

"Making this proposal epic fo' them."

With a huge grin on his face, Colby said, "I know we ain't finna do no school age shit ... like we did when we first asked them out?"

217

With a smile on my face, I said, "Only if you cool wit' it."

"Mane, we too grown fo' that shit. I'm twenty-six an' you are twenty-eight, do you think it's wise we propose to our women … in the manner that you want? Do you know how childish it would be?" He laughed.

"Yep, but it's also a Fernando an' Colby thing."

"True, but still though, shouldn't we do this solo?"

Sighing heavily, I said, "Yeah, but I want us to do what we did when we first asked them out."

"I swear you are one strange ass nigga."

From his tone, I knew that my cousin wasn't with it; thus, I made him see why we should. "When I wanted Zariah to be my girlfriend, who asked?"

"Me."

"When you wanted Nene to be yo' girlfriend, who asked?"

"You."

"When you wanted to have a baby wit' Nene, who brought up that topic of her gettin' off birth control?"

"You."

"Every time I pissed off Zariah or somethin' was off between us, who fixed it?"

"Me."

"Who *always* fixes yo' fuck ups?"

Laughing, Colby said, "Okay, nigga, I get it. I get it. Basically, you want me to cry so that no one else will watch you shed tears?"

"Exactly. Now, you really get it," I told him with a smile on my face.

"You are one strange ass nigga, I swear. When do you want to do this?"

"Right now," I announced as I handed him the box with Zariah's ring in it.

Tucking it into his back pocket, he gave me Nene's ring and said, "Alright. So, like always I go first?"

"Nope, this time ... I'm going to go first. That way I can live up to my word of you bullyin' me," I told him as we embraced in a loving, manly hug.

"By the way, thanks fo' that."

"No problem," I told him as we pulled apart.

"Let's get them to cryin', shall we?"

"We shall."

"Is there any song requests you want to play in the background when I drop down on Zariah?" I asked.

"See, that's why I fuck wit' you, nigga ... I didn't think of that ... hell yes, um ... R. Kelly's 'Forever'."

"Bet," he replied as he thumbed through his phone.

"Do you have a song in mind?" I asked.

"Selecting it now so all you have to do is press play."

As we walked out of room, my heart raced as I anticipated the look on their faces. Nene and Zariah were true ride or die females. They weren't with the street shit; they wanted legit men that could provide and protect them. My cousin and I couldn't give that to them while we ran the streets—only selling drugs. After the shit we had been in, we saw that now was the perfect time to give them our last names.

Stepping into the living room, I briefly looked around the room with a smile on my face. Everyone was coupled up as they chatted about different things. The talking didn't stop until I dropped down on one knee in front of Nene as she slapped her hands over her mouth and shook her head.

"Oh my Goddd!" Zariah happily yelled while hugging a crying Nene.

"Oh, shit! Oh, shit! They still on that childish ass shit!" Auntie Maryann stated happily, causing everyone to laugh.

"Wow, what in the hell is really going on?" Markesha asked with bucked eyes.

Getting my shit together, I retrieved the empty box and grabbed her left hand as Jagged Edge "I Gotta Be" played from Colby's phone.

"Nene, you been there fo' a nigga mo' times than I can count. I don't see a day without you being in my life. I can't fathom you not cursin' me out or blowin' up my phone if I don't respond within fo' point five seconds. I need you mo' than you think I do ... you an' our son completes me. There will *never* be any other that was made just fo' me. I *need* you an' only you. I promise you that I will be better than before. You are my queen, an' I'm more than ready to be yo' knight in shining armor. Sheneka Laniya Russe, will you do me the honor of givin' you my last name an' many mo' babies to come ... 'til we old an' gray?"

Standing, I stepped back a few inches. Hopping to her feet with a huge smile on her tear-stained face, Nene ran towards Colby all the while happily saying, "Yes. Yes, I'll marry you, wit' yo' childish ass!"

"Congratulations!" everyone shouted as Colby dropped to one knee and placed the ring on his happy woman's finger.

"I love you, Nene. I've loved you since the first day I placed my eyes on you and you cursed me out. That was the day I knew I was going to marry you once I mentally grew up."

As they embraced and kissed, Zariah strolled towards me and said, "Y'all so damn sneaky. Why you didn't tell me that he was going to propose today?"

"Because it was a secret," I voiced softly before planting a kiss on her forehead.

We resumed enjoying our morning with our family. Zariah had no idea what was coming her way, and that's why I was glad that Colby waited. I didn't want to overwhelm them in one setting; I wanted Zariah to be caught off guard like Nene was. That made the surprise just that much better.

Thirty minutes later, Gun'em and Colby were in the corner talking. The time was approaching for Zariah to accept my proposal; a nigga's hands were sweaty as fuck. My heart seemed as if it was going to run out my chest. I hadn't been this nervous since I stood behind my locker—the day after I lost my virginity to Zariah—so that Colby could ask her to be my girlfriend.

That foolish ass cousin of mine sauntered away from Gun'em as if he was a pimp, causing everyone to laugh.

"I see now, y'all going to be goofy ass boys until the end, huh?" Nanna questioned, laughing.

"Yes, ma'am," Colby said as he walked towards the back porch.

Too much attention was on him; thus, he had to go on whatever plan he had in his mind. I couldn't wait to see what that damn nut was going to do.

"What is you finna do stupid now, Son?" Uncle Colby asked, chuckling.

Standing tall, Colby turned around and rubbed the non-existent beard and said, "Uncle Colby, sometimes a man gotta do what a man gotta do."

"My nigga!" I yelled, jumping to my feet.

I couldn't lie as if the nigga didn't do a good impersonation of me. Everyone in the room was in laughter while shaking their head.

Walking like me, Colby sauntered towards the kitchen and Zariah busted out laughing and said, "You get on my nerves, Colby."

Colby made a noise with his mouth and dropped to one knee as R. Kelly's 'Forever' played on the phone. Applauses and cheers filled the cabin as my auntie began to cry.

"Baby, we been rockin' wit' me since kindergarten. We have been inseparable since then. There hasn't been a soul that could keep my love away from you or make me disloyal to what we've had since day one. I *am* not goin' to spend my life without you an' our son. I *need* y'all mo' than life itself. I *need* to grow old an' wrinkly wit' you. I *need* to have the white picket fence, a batch of churren runnin' 'round the front yard, an' all of yo' lovin'. I *need* to continue receivin' yo' wonderful love that you bestow upon me. MaZariah Chloe Nash, will you do me the honor of allowin' me to give you my last name as I continue to be yo' knight in shining armor?"

As tears dripped down my woman's face while she looked at me, Colby stood and wiped his face.

"Yes, I'll marry you, Fernando!" Zariah cried as she ran into my arms.

Before I rained kisses on her, I dropped to one knee and said, "*That* beautiful, special night when we were in the seventh grade, I told you that I belonged to you an' I meant it. I'm going to tell you, again … I belong to you, MaZariah Chloe Nash."

The newly engaged women hugged each other as everyone applauded and clapped. Once the shouting and applauds ceased, Gun'em cleared his throat. With our eyes on him, he waited a while before speaking.

"Um, y'all know I been in them streets fo' a while. I think it's time fo' me to retire along wit' my partners. I've always valued the love, dedication, an' loyalty between Colby an' Nene, Grinch an' Zariah, an' Uncle Colby an' Auntie Maryann. That type of love I *need* in my life. The type of love that make you come home before the street lights come on." He chuckled, causing us to nod our heads.

Continuing, Gun'em nervously said, "When the smoke clears, Shardya, I would love to take you on a date an' properly love you the right way. So, Shardya, will you accept my future date proposal?"

Nodding her head with a smile on her face, she hugged Gun'em and said, "Yes, I will accept your future date proposal."

When I woke up this morning, I knew that my family and I would have a great beginning, but I didn't know great would turn into spectacular. Our lives were going to be forever changed, and I knew not a soul in the living room didn't give a damn as long as it was a positive change without any street drama.

"To new beginnings wit' happiness, love, an' a family bond like none other!" I shouted with Zariah in my arms.

"To new beginnings with happiness, love, and a family bond like none other!" everyone shouted while clapping and smiling.

About the Author

TN Jones resides in the state of Alabama with her daughter. Growing up, TN Jones always had a passion for and writing, which led her to

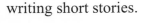 writing short stories.

In 2015, TN Jones began working on her first book, *Disloyal: Revenge of a Broken Heart*, which was previously titled, *Passionate Betrayals*.

TN Jones writes in the following fictional Urban/Interracial genres: Women's/Romance, Mystery/Suspense, Dark Erotica/Erotica, Street Lit/Chick Lit, and Paranormal.

Published novels by TN Jones: *Disloyal: Revenge of a Broken Heart, Disloyal 2-3: A Woman's Revenge, A Sucka in Love for a Thug, If You'll Give Me Your Heart 1-2, By Any Means: Going Against the Grain 1-2, The Sins of Love: Finessing the Enemies 1-3, Caught Up In a D-Boy's Illest Love 1-3, Choosing To Love A Lady Thug 1-4, Is This Your Man, Sis: Side Piece Chronicles, Just You and Me: A Magical Love Story, Jonesin' For A Boss Chick: A Montgomery Love Story* and *That Young Hood Love 1-2.*

Upcoming novels by TN Jones*: Give Me What I Want, If My Walls Could Talk, The Lost Dhampir Princess*, and more.

Thank you for reading ***The Grinch That Stole My Heart***. Leave an honest review under the book title on Amazon or Goodreads.

For future book details, please visit any of the links below:

Amazon Author page: https://www.amazon.com/tnjones666

Facebook: https://www.facebook.com/novelisttnjones/

Goodreads: https://www.goodreads.com/author/show/14918893.TN_Jones:

Instagram: https://www.instagram.com/tnjones666

Twitter: https://twitter.com/TNJones666.

You are welcome to **email** her: tnjones666@gmail.com

Chat with her daily in the **Facebook** group: *Its Just Me…TN Jones.*

Did You Enjoy This Book?

Leaving an honest review is beneficial for me as an author. It is one of the most potent tools used as I seek attention for my books. Receiving feedback from readers will increase my chances of reaching other readers that haven't read a book by me. Word of mouth is a great way to spread the news of a book that you've enjoyed.

With that being said, once you reach this page, please scroll to the review section and leave an honest review. Be sure to click the box for Goodreads as well as Amazon. As always, thank you for taking a chance on allowing me to provide you with quality entertainment.

Peace and Blessings, Loves!